The Midtown Express

Samual Baptiste

(The Midtown Express)

ISBN: 978-0-615-80458-3

Dedication

For those who have hurt others and have found, or believe you will find, forgiveness-- you are blessed. For you know serenity now.

For those who believe you have not hurt others and have not sought forgiveness-- well.........

Foreword

Dear reader,

Please note that this book should be considered as a work of fiction; as largely, am I. If I have overstepped my boundaries in writing it, please forgive me. For I presume to offend almost all, and receive criticism in kind. But I do ask for the same spirit of forgiveness for which this memoir has been written.

Also, please forgive a fool for pretending to be a scholar. For if scholars are learned men of discipline and fools just pretend to be, then I must confess myself to be aligned with the latter. But being a self confessed fool does allow one certain leeway….

For one, I must confess that you will indeed find a myriad of errors in this book; these errors that should frustrate both the editors of your world and your "established" theologians. And that just makes me smile.

But take solace in the fact that what I may lack in the formal mechanics of my writing will be just as audacious as my misinterpretations of classical theology. So again, keeping forgiveness and plurality of thought in mind, please enjoy my recollections.

-- *Sam*

Introduction

Why this has happened, I don't know. But I have been granted an opportunity-- a very rare opportunity, to tell my story. And as you'll find out, I'm rarely one to turn down an opportunity. You see, I'm no prophet or profiteer, just a wayward soul trying finding his way with a faltering moral compass.

But this book is based…somewhat…on the facts of my existence. However, even I must recognize that the marching progress of father time may have "over inflated" these facts ever so slightly. But I suppose that's one of the traps of our very unique human nature.

It all started long ago. It was late at night and I really should have been paying more attention…….

Chapter One

Eternal Rain and a Hidden Agenda

"Father, I gotta go. Nope, I'll see everyone soon.....Yeah, I've got another call beeping in now." Sam enjoyed calling his Dad by a more formal name. He found it ironic as the two had grown so close later in life. "Call ya tomorrow."

"*I should NOT be multitasking while driving in the rain.*" Sam thought as he pressed buttons on his phone. "Sam here." He answered tersely. It was his standard business answer when he didn't know who was calling. "Hi!" she responded loudly. As he cradled the phone on his shoulder, he silently cursed his luck twice; Once for losing his ear piece and once again for not checking caller ID. He surely would have avoided this call and avoided the upcoming drama.

"*Offer thee a way out Lord...*" He silently and mockingly prayed. "*How 'bout a quick meteor strike to the head?*" "Uhh... hey, what's up?" He muttered. He knew his voice must've sounded very tired. It had been a long, long day and this B.S. was the last thing he needed. Answering this call from his ex girlfriend would absolutely add to that stress.

"The weather is horrible—I can't really talk now. I'm just heading to the house now. No..... no way I can't make it out tonight, how 'bout next time? I'll bring the wife and we can all meet and hang out."

Most people wouldn't have even answered, but ever since the break up years ago, he had tried to maintain some sort of friendship with her. Something to offset the pain that he'd felt when others had broken his heart and he, theirs. But really he was just playing out the game.

"Precious Sammy-- You always find every excuse in the book." Her reply dripped with sarcasm. "I just want to hang out as friends." "*Yeah, right.*" He thought. "*Here we go again.*"

Blood began boiling in his voice. "Look, we would be happy to …" But he just let it go. He knew the frustration in his voice was beginning to show. He was trying to let her down easily and just go on without betraying his usual anger, but this was getting old quick. He started to fume as he maneuvered the Jeep down the seemingly endless Carolina side road. The bravado that he'd learned from years in the Marines had left him with just enough over confidence to be able to drive, talk and adjust the radio all at the same time.

Of all the lies he had told, she knew that this was just another one, as did he. But he'd rather lie a little now than to hurt her more later. The last girl he tried to date before his wife had really thrown him for a loop as did the one before. And he was determined to be a better person than them. But right now, he just had to get her off the phone. "Look, we'd be happy to have you guys over." He insincerely mumbled.

"*Thy divine karma really is a son of a….*" he thought and looked up. While not an overly religious man, Sam did have a bad habit of mockingly praying out of frustration, not thanks. And this situation was just another perfect example of how his sins had indeed come back to haunt him. But he was determined not to treat her like "She who shall not be named" did him. As he stewed over his unfortunate circumstance, Sam became immune to the fast moving world outside. Quickly, from the corner of his eye, he spotted a massive brown blur.

"Son of a…. !!!" He yelled out. The beautiful brown buck careened across the wet road in front of him. A quick shot of adrenaline surged through him.

"Jesus, that was close!" He yelled into the phone. "Look, I almost just crashed and the rain's a little heavy tonight. I really need to go." He thought that she might get the obvious blurt, but she went on like nothing ever happened. Sam angrily hit the end button—problem solved. He immediately felt better and resumed his drive.

In general, he enjoyed the summer's nightly coastal sprinkles. They were usually a welcome feeling against the blistering heat of the day. But the marshy humidity was working extra hard against the old Jeep's air conditioning tonight. "*OK, back to normal. I can do this. At least the road side swampy scenery is cool--. Kinda creepy really.*" He thought with a smile as his tired mind began to wander again. In the background, he could hear still hear her talking. "*Unbelievable.*" He thought.

Union and Confederate cemeteries dotted the road side as he flew by. He loved the history of this area and scanned from side to side to see the blurry, gray headstones. He tiredly looked down to see if he could adjust the fan even higher. The constant whirr of the air conditioning droned on into oblivion in the background.

With a renewed sense of confidence and serenity, he continued winding down the lazy two lane road. These night drives always seemed a little more soothing than his usual day trips. However, they also added to the drowsiness that the evening's rot-gut gas station coffee just wasn't remedying.

The rain's rhythmic pitter-patter continuously washed the Jeep's windshield clean. The stress of the day started to drip off with the rhythmic rain. As he fell deeper into relaxation, his eyelids started to close. Shimmering thoughts of Christmas and Christmas mass filled his head. *"Odd,"* he half-thought… *Christmas mass? It's been years…..*"

Masses said in Latin from his youth began to cloud his head as the world flew by his half opened eyes. His eyes became heavier and heavier and his breathing became more and more relaxed. As the Jeep started to swerve, Sam sat up and startled himself with a defiant shot of self realization, "Wake up!"

Throughout the world of dream and reality, he tried to force himself awake. He tried to focus on the NPR talk show he had droning in the background. The car started to swerve again…..

"*Today Sam! Wake up!*" he berated himself silently. He sat up abruptly and rolled down the window. It may have been raining, but he needed to wake up. As he glanced down to change the channel on the glowing blue screen below, it suddenly flashed a brilliant white.

And for a split second, a quick and very dreaded realization of the situation filled his mind.

All the world went white as acid stung his stomach as two headlights came at him fast. He jolted the steering wheel away from the headlights, but it was too late. The whole world seemed for just a second to be as bright as two suns. The ensuing Hell hurt for only a second as the car flipped violently.

As his head snapped around, he noticed almost whimsically how everything happened so slowly. The scene turned into a silent film that seemed almost funny to watch.

"Holy souls in….." He was still blurred in half reality mixed with the semi-dream of Christmas Mass. That semi vision was ended by a real, physical object-- A large chrome menace. It was the massive truck's bumper flying through the windshield that was his last real clear vision of this Earth. The blackout was quick; the ringing in his head endless.

Purgatorial ringing hummed in his ears and seemed to last forever. This wasn't exactly an unusual sensation for Sam. As a child, years of suffering from low blood sugar blackouts had prepared him for this...experience. *"Honey, wake up."* He could hear his mother's comforting words droning softly through the Christmas mass dream in his head." *"It's OK Mom."* He thought dreamily, *"I just passed out again."* A smile crossed his unconscious face.

Chapter Two

Rest.

Sam's world spun like a washing machine. Chrome metal mixed with glass and earth filled the void that was once air that surrounded him. As the Jeep tumbled, the roof collapsed and the glass encrusted earth tore through Sam's exposed skin. Metal merged with bone; bone with earth.

Finally, the Jeep rested on its broken side and neither the Jeep nor Sam moved an inch. Slowly, Sam regained consciousness. "*Just breath through it and you'll be fine Sam….Let's do this again.*"But this time it was different; there was no complete soaking of sweat, no nausea to overcome.

As he came through, the ringing in his ears became a roaring like the ocean waves that he and his daughter loved so very much. An intense pressure overtook his skull. He felt his stomach turning as viciously sharp pains ripped through his entire body. Vomit and blood filled his mouth.

In the open storm drain directly below him, Sam watched the storm water rising slowly. It was mixing quickly with gasoline and his own life's blood. Warm and almost soothing at first, the liquid actually seemed to be like a sheet, wrapping him as the deep pain began to dull. His eyesight blurred, but returned for just a minute. He could see flashing lights in the distance.

"*Hurry*." He thought through intense pain.

"Hurry." Sam muttered as he held out his arm.

Closer and closer the sirens roared until finally stopping their raging howls when they pulled alongside. Through bloodied eyes, Sam could see the firemen and another figure running down the embankment. Only the dirty MACK truck baseball cap identified this man as the truck driver that must've hit him. He and the firemen were now frantically trying to pull Sam from the now smoking car.

Looking dazedly up out of the wrecked car, Sam noticed a tall wooden steeple and headstones just to the side. How ironic, he thought: "*Church. I skipped that last week-- Perfect.*"

"Those legs are broken, be careful." One of the firemen commented coldly. "You're going to be alright buddy. Hang in there."

But Sam could barely hear him as the merciless rain now pounded steadily from above. The fireman noted quietly that Sam's blood was already streaming from his nose, mouth and chest. Sam began to struggle for air. His punctured chest was broken in ways that he couldn't even begin to comprehend. Even the slightest move of his suspended, sideways body shot pain through him that made him want to vomit.

From the back of the Jeep, the familiar smell of gasoline also began to get stronger and stronger. The seat belt dutifully held him just inches above the rising water in the ditch. Panic began to set in for his saviors. But not for Sam, who was now far too in shock to do, or feel, much of anything.

For Sam, the reflection of the flashing lights from the gathering emergency vehicles danced for him beautifully in the tepid pool below. It was almost… amusing. And with every passing moment, the pain was lessening.

Another group of firemen arrived and ran to the totaled Jeep. Their yellow reflective jackets already slick in the pouring rain. The lead fireman, a man of twenty years experience, knew things weren't going well. His graying mustache, scars and roughen hands betrayed his years running into harm's way.

He noted Sam's whitening skin and ordered the new crew to work faster. "C'mon dammit! Get those jaws out and start cutting!" He knew that within Sam's lungs, less and less oxygen was being processed… his chances slipping away. Sam's breathing became shallower and his skin began to turn an ashen gray. The two young men and the trucker began to work furiously. A large fire extinguisher was set to put out the small fire. It spewed forth foam that now added another objection to what should have been a quiet evening on a quiet Carolina road side.

As Sam started to slip in and out of consciousness, he began feeling life's cruel ocean's waves crashing in his head again; waves that silently tumbled only in his ears.

They too would start to recede and would eventually be replaced by the constant, almost electronic, hum of the void. The hum that he'd known was a forbearer to the black abyss he'd visited all too often in his lifetime.

"My Family…." He murmured as he started drifting away.

His blood spattered muttering became slurred to the point of absurdity. Coughing and spitting, broken teeth fell into the dirty storm water below. As the trucker and the firemen continued cutting and wrestling to set Sam free, he momentarily regained consciousness and locked eyes with the burly trucker. He was only able to mutter softly –"My… family. Plea..."

But the merciful void took over Sam's head. The images of the firemen left him as well; the odd smell of gasoline, burning clothes and fresh rain gone with it. His pain lessened as quickly as his pulse. These final events unfolded like they do for every mortal in this world. The widening pupils were an all too familiar sight for the firefighters.

Sam stared forward with his open, surprised eyes. His pain stopped. Everything became very silent. His last sound was that of the muffled crying of the truck driver. Nothing; sweet, sweet nothing.

Then, the lifting began.

Slowly, Sam became aware that he was now oddly conscious again and incredibly, outside of his own body. Looking down, he gently rose to view the entire scene below. A beautiful, sparkling, crystal white ring gently surrounded the entire area. He controlled absolutely nothing.

He watched with fascination and noticed that the police were now there too; frantic black and orange motions of defeated saviors still working to save his broken, dead body. One of the young firefighters was half way in the Jeep and pumping at his chest slowly.

"*My God.*" He thought. "*What's happening?*" The semi driver sat a few feet away beneath him, sobbing openly. His head held between his shaking hands. The burly man was softly begging somebody, anybody, to forgive him. Sam looked down from a slight distance and looked directly into his own open eyes. "S*trange.*" He thought calmly. He had no control. He was only calm-- very, very calm.

He only felt…. the rising. As he gently floated, he also began to notice movement all around. A strange darkness that began swirling in the swamp entrenched trees that edged ever closer. The dark mass wickedly approached and with it an intense feeling of fear. This… fear was accompanied by a growling, angry wind that seemed to actually laugh as it danced through the trees.

Something, some… thing….. was approaching from all directions. Something that made him "feel"…. terrified. Even though he couldn't see "it"—he sure as Hell could feel it.

The absolute blackness began slowly swirling beneath. It covered the scene below in a sickening black fog that the moving people didn't seem to notice as they continued their work. He tried to yell to warn them, but nothing came out. He wanted to run, but he just…. rose. He needed to warn the people below, but they just continued working in the sick blanket of anger. They worked in a flurry of activity that the blackness didn't seem to mind either.

As the swirls rose upward, this absurd darkness began reaching *for* him.

Not reaching his feet, because, he noted madly, he had no feet. No real body at all, just his vision looking down at the horrid mass swirling ever faster below. The dark fog seemed almost to harden in places. Forming its own lengthy, sickening form.

It took on an almost human form-- almost. The foggy shape gelled where a body should be and a blank oval where a face should. As he watched helplessly, a thin arm of…something came reaching for him. An extreme feeling of sadness and terror overcame him as it neared.

As he watched the horror transforming below, a soothing warmth also slowly formed above. Without sound, sparkling bright lights rained from above. It was if he was the center in a synchronized dance between two unknown forces. Floating between these forces, he was soon saturated with a rushing, train-pounding, feeling that flowed through his entire being from above.

The cascading lights from above streamed into a myriad of small, colorful rivers. These rivers flowed together around him everywhere. They pierced the darkness, enveloping Sam's world.

For the first time, Sam could also hear. He indeed heard something. Confusion set in, but one thing was for certain. He heard the increasing volume of people screaming.

It was a deep, raging scream that came from the blackness.

As the screams intensified, the silent, warm light above also continued to surround him. But the black sickness from below resisted and also started to encircle him. The two forces mixed. As he continued to rise, the colors mixed with, and finally overtook, the black. An intense feeling of safety set in; much like that of a child resting in his parent's arms. Euphoria tingled his entire spirit and calm danced in his soul like the lights that now danced all around him. The sadness and terror drifted away as the intensity of the light strengthened around him.

Then the slow rising stopped.

A quick, jolting shift moved him forward and upward at incredible speed. The light formed into a tunnel of even more vibrant colors. As he moved quickly up the now forming tunnel, it seemed as though a rainbow itself was transporting him.

Warmth and happiness kissed him as he moved at this incredible speed forward. As he travelled, he was actually able to look into each stream of light. The deeper he looked, the more he "saw" or was aware of memories of his life. It was almost as though he were reliving each one of them. Each hue of the stream carried in it a different life experience.

As he looked further, he could see behind the streams. He could see the actual cosmos flying by. Unknown solar systems colliding and breathing as he travelled. Bright colors of planets and stars that he could barely withstand. The whole world was just… living.

But the rivers surrounding him would not be ignored. As he looked deeper into them, he could see that the lightest white, red, orange and yellow streams reflected such happy memories: His daughter's birth, his wedding, his friends and so many times happy with his family. But as he jolted through the tunnel, he also noticed the darker streams. The purples and blues indicating much darker times: Unfaithfulness, lying, cheating, war, deception…..

The streams stopped and he merged into an open white light. This "space" in front of him surrounded an icon that he knew only too well. The wood of timbers seemed to seep blood from its very pores.

He seemed to be alone but deep down, he knew better. For behind him he could now feel "it" again. The same cold sickness he felt from the dark of the woods. He dared not turn around when he heard a slight snicker.

He felt the sadness tugging from behind. Letting out a desperate cry, Sam tried to "run" forward. An incredible fire completely and instantly engulfed his world. He swam in massive flames that rolled to the command of an unknown conductor. He felt the fire in his whole being.

It was a Hellish heat that completely overtook him. The pain was just too much to comprehend. It seared through his entire being. But it did not burn. "Help me." Sam pleaded.

A deep voice whispered in the darkness and he drifted into a deep sleep; A rare sleep that happens without dreams. The kind of sleep that only the very young are blessed with.

"Rest..."

Chapter Three

Grant Unto Them a Light

He slept hard. A deep slumber that seemed to last for years. Eventually, a slow, shimmering white light crept over his darkness. Slowly, he became "conscious" and slowly awoke. "*Do I smell Roses*?" Sam thought dreamily.

As he laid there, he slowly became more and more coherent. He could smell the familiar pungent aroma of the disinfectant overcoming the roses. He felt the cold crispness of new sheets. "*Great. Another God damned hospital*" he thought angrily. "*Here we go again.*" He tried to remember the dream that he'd just had, but it was difficult.

He could feel a satin cut of cloth covered his eyes. '*That's new.*" He mused. He wanted to lift it, wanted to know what was happening. "*What did I have? One of those freaky Shirley McClain out of body experiences? No one was going to believe this!*" He thought.

Then an odd realization came to him. '*Wait. Where's the pain? Where was the blood that filled my mouth? What about the light? The tunnel? The dark? Damn, I must've been out for an eternity.*"

" Damn, I must've been out for a while." He muttered aloud.

"Don't move too much." A male voice said sternly. The male voice surprised Sam. "You've had quite a trip." It was a reassuring voice; almost kind, yet very resolved. "You're in a hospital." he said with a slight humor. "Or at least a version of one."

"What?" Sam hazily responded. "I thought I was dead. What hospital am I in? What day is it? Where's my family? Man, I thought I was a goner."

"Well, that's kind of a long story. You've actually been "a goner" for quite a long time." The doctor replied. "*A coma*?" Sam thought. "I thought I may have bitten the bullet or something. Hey, whoever you are, can I take this eye thing off my eyes? Was I in a coma or something? You a doc?"

"Of course you can," the stranger's voice continued. "Look, be careful. Don't sit up too quickly or be abrupt in any way. You have to get used to your new….. situation."

"Ok," Sam said sleepily. "But I don't understand. I feel great. I just need to get out of here." He slowly lifted the satin. His eyes took a second to readjust, the bright lights harsh at first, then softening.

A few feet away, he could see the figure in front of him taking shape. The fuzzy figure slowly solidified into a very familiar person. "I've s*een this guy before, must be a local doc."* Sam thought.

"You feeling OK?" the doctor asked. His white coat seemed to be flawless in whiteness. An oddly large stethoscope dangled from his neck. "*Weird, I must still be on pain meds.*" He thought. The doctor's sharp nose and grey eyes were supported by a short almost military type haircut. His body also seemed very fit, filling out the coat even under the light cotton.

He had a slight smirk on his face. "W*hat is that in his mouth? Tobacco? A chew? Since when did doctors chew tobacco???"* Sam mused. He started to straighten up in his bed and went on, "Where am I Doc? I remember crashing, the light, then… I'm here."

The doctor leaned in closer. "*EXACTLY* what do you remember? Tell me everything." He went on to tell the doctor about the accident, the pain, the rising, the dark figure, the tunnel, the light, the cross. "Good." Said the doctor. "That's about what I figured."

"You figured? Doc, what the Hell's going on here?"

"Not what the Hell." the doctor replied. "What the "middle" actually… or……Purgatory….or at least, your version of it" The absurdity of the statement hit Sam hard. This guy was screwing around with him and Sam just didn't appreciate it.

He took a second to let his mind think before his mouth spoke. He'd always prided himself on careful reasoning. "OK doc, I'll play your reindeer games. Did my brother put you up to this? Where the Hell is that schmuck?"

The doctor quickly cut him off. "Look, here's the deal- you are, and I'm going to over simplify the situation, very, very dead. So take a second, internalize what I've said and just… breathe."

"Breathe? Doc, How can I breathe if I'm dead? Nice try, but I'm getting a little pissed and right now I'd like to get the Hell out of here." As he was saying this, he wondered why he wasn't as mad internally as he said he was externally. He was saying all the right angry things, but the anger just wasn't….there.

As he pretended to be overly angry, he glanced down at his attire. He was wearing a nice white satin bath robe. Complete with his initials on the left breast pocket. He also noticed something quite peculiar when he glanced at his fingers, hands and arms. He was in absolutely perfect shape; the scars on his hands from years of hard labor were gone.

He even had clipped nails-- He never had clipped nails. They were all chewed down because of the nervousness. All of that could be explained by the coma, but the broken bones that gnarled some of his fingers were gone as well. There's no way that months in a coma would do that. "Oh no….." The first hint of truth became apparent. "Oh no…"

The truth in front of him was hard to handle. He hated not having control. He'd lived his life the best he could and often he failed, but at least he'd always maintained at least the illusion of control. He looked up at the doctor and wanted to be sad, but he was not. The rush of truth came at him hard and fast.

He wanted to cry, but the tears wouldn't come. He wanted to be angry, but that old familiar feeling just wasn't there. He wanted to worry, but it just kept… slipping out of his grasp. He looked up completely lost in unknown emotions. He wanted to be sad but only….. felt?…. content. It didn't make any sense.

"Damn doc…." Slowly, Sam surrendered. "Damn. Damn. I think I'm really dead. Look, I want to be sad and angry but….I….I can't."

"I know." the doctor said softly. "This will take a little while for you to get used to. But if you try hard enough, you can get sad; sad, angry and mad all over again. You just can't do it now because of your recent closeness to God." Sam opened his eyes a little wider. *"God?"* Sam thought.

The helplessness of his situation was simply overpowering. With a sigh of resignation, he managed to utter, "So Heaven is a hospital bed? No…. if I'm dead I should be floating around for eternity like a gumball or somethin'."

The absurdity of the statement made both men look at each other for a quick second. The doctor sat back and tilted his head with the quizzical tilt of a very confused German Sheppard. A smile crept on his face. It didn't seem that long ago when the doctor himself was that confused. He almost envied the poor guy-- Almost.

"Again" the doctor restated. "It's because of your recent closeness to God that you cannot express your grief. Just let all this… sink in…. for a sec."

Sam confusedly looked around. He did have his faith, but it wasn't as strong as it should have been. He'd completely lost it for a long time during his rebellious years-- Years that ultimately cost him his marriage. But if he was truly dead and not swimming in a pool of fire, then something must be alright.

But none of it felt right. He wasn't even a *good* Catholic. His differences with the church didn't even allow him to *legally* go to confession or communion. He'd chosen her over that; No way God sent her to him and then sent the priests to tell him it wasn't right. Score: Wife one; Church zero.

So there's no way he should be here now. By all accounts of what he read and was told, he should be swimming around in a pool of fire, with Ol' Scratch poking him every few minutes with a pitchfork just for fun.

While the insanity of the new situation flowed through his head, at least some sense of reality eventually dawned on him. "Wait. Where's Grandma and Grandpa? My aunt and uncle? Abe freakin' Lincoln?" *'My God,"* he thought… I just made a friggin joke; your family is all alone and you just made a joke." The first real hint of sadness entered his mind.

The doctor read his emotions and sat next to the bed. "You will start to feel a rush of emotions from happiness to almost…sadness. You'll have moments of clarity and confusion. Take your time with this- you have an eternity to figure it out."

"Eternity." He weakly asked aloud. "No way… How do I survive without my family? How will they survive without me? Who will watch over them?" His thoughts now portrayed in his eyes as well as his voice. Sam's voice started to crack.

"You will." the young doctor replied. "It will be hard on them at first, and they will suffer some of the same depression that you suffered from in your life, but your family will survive-- Just as you did. But they have a long road to travel before they are with you again."

"Besides" The doctor emphasized, "You will have the ability to look in on them and perhaps even help them. From time to time, of course."

"What do you mean?" Sam replied confusedly. "I don't even know exactly where I am. Look, I'm so…. I have no idea who you are or where to go from here."

"But that's why I'm here." The doctor replied with a reassuring smile. "I'm here to get you through this. The hospital bed and fancy schmancy satin eye coverings were actually of your making…"

Sam paused. "How… is it my doing? This really makes no flippin sense, Jesu….." He quickly stopped. If this truly was….well….not Hell, he better not take the Lord's name in vain. "*You never know who may be listening….*" Sam thought absurdly.

The doctor laughed at Sam's attempt. His laugh was a deep…almost familiar…. laugh. The doctor's grey eyes twinkled with a knowing that Sam just couldn't place his finger on. "OK" the doctor said flatly. "Let's start at the beginning. You were a Christian in your life on Earth, yes?"

"I suppose…Yes." He replied. "I went to Catholic school as forced labor as a boy and finally escaped to public high school. I did "stray" from the church in my military and later married years. It wasn't until my divorce and subsequent heart breaks, did I go back to the church."

Sam continued confusedly. "But my, I guess you could call them, "active years in the church" were far outweighed by my time *away* from the church." Sam knew he was starting to ramble. He took a second to try to regain his composure.

"Hell doc." Sam's voice now quieter, "Even back in church, I was relegated to a lesser class of sorts. But I just couldn't *not* marry her, ya know? Both of us divorced or not. There's just no way I should be sitting here now. Someone screwed up the accounts receivable books, Doc."

"*Again with the jokes.*" Sam thought. It felt like his usual way of dealing with stress might just bite him in the ass this time. The doctor openly chuckled.

"Look" the doctor replied. "To oversimplify things greatly, whether you like it or not, you are in a form of.....Purgatory. How you deal with that depends on how you look at it. But I can tell you this, only through God's grace did you get this far. That's how we all get into.... This place... only through God's grace, get it?

The trick is, not only are you judged, but you also have to decide whether to accept God's grace or not. Well, that's usually how it happens. There are certain situations that overrule this accommodation. Take for example, murderers who haven't repented, rapists who haven't repented, etc.... You know, the real hard asses.

Look, it kinda comes down to this: If your penance in life isn't adequate to wash away your sins, then Heavenly access is not a given. But, you can be given the chance to wash them away here. And, if you work on it long enough here, then one day you may actually get into Heaven.

But even in Purgatory and in Heaven there are different.....how would you think of it.....levels? Not physical levels, like a reverse Dante, but individual spiritual levels of the soul itself.

"Spiritual levels? Purgatory? What?" Sam asked.

"Yep. See, basically, you chose Jesus via Christianity as your savior and then to ultimately be your judge and so on. Because of this internalized belief system, you stood before him and he judged you. You don't remember any of this because it happens in a fraction of a second. You probably saw an icon of your belief. You may have even felt the "foul one" tugging behind you. But ultimately your "good deeds", acceptance, forgiveness and life's lessons outweighed those sins that you have committed against God and others and luckily, you're here..."

The smile on the doctor's face reassured Sam, but this was all happening so damn fast. "Look doc, I…."

But the doctor cut him off. "Sam, ultimately Jesus judged you on the Heaven, Hell or Purgatory issue. In the end, Jesus decided no Hell for you, but no Heaven either. Now you're here and are somewhere on the ol' Purgatory scale and you gotta get yourself cleaned up. Got it?"

"No." Sam honestly replied. "This is all so much. This isn't happening. How could it? I'm not ready!"

"Sam. It has happened. You are here." The doctor lessened his voice. "*This really is a lot. I've got to slow down.*"

Sitting in silence, they both stumbled for the next thing to say.

Starting to accept his fate, Sam tried to use his familiar fallback- humor.

"Well, I guess that I avoided hanging out with Hitler in Hell…Seems folks have always been a lousy judge of my character; I just never thought it would keep me *out* of Hell."

The doc locked eyes with him and they both chuckled together for the first time. The doctor took the opportunity to continue. "Sam, your life had worth. Even though you were a sinner, you had learned from those mistakes and had tried to repent. So that's why you're here now.

You were granted to be in God's presence, but not in his Heavenly presence. Only a…. pure soul… gets that. So you get a lesser version of Heaven. You simply aren't pure enough yet to move up. Hell, you may never be." The doc was smiling as he said it, but Sam knew that there was always a little truth in every joke.

"I get what you're saying doc. And I know that I should be feeling… relieved, but I still want to "feel" sad. I mean, sadder than I am. I mean, I'm dead! I don't have my family! But all I really mostly feel is…… content. This is just crazy." They doctor sat in silence and patiently waited for the rant to pass.

Sam stared sullenly at the doctor and also glanced at his surroundings. "Ok." Sam said with resignation. "So what's up with the hospital?"

The doctor smiled softly as he spoke with soft authority. "When you are ready, you and I will leave this hospital. I'm just as curious as you are to see what's outside."

"Wait." Sam thought slyly. That old feeling of "getting over" coming back to him. "I should be able to produce a bottle of Jim Beam, a rocket ship to get home, and a few dozen nurses in mini-skirts. Yet I don't see them magically appearing. So what's up with that doc?"

The doctor frowned in response, the weight of his voice apparent. "Those are not *needs* my friend, those are desires. And desires, even here....No, especially here, can be extremely dangerous. Don't think that Heaven cannot be lost, Sam. Although it is rare, Heaven and even Purgatory, can sift through your hands like grains of sand. Leaving only one other option for your soul. And you don't want to go there."

Sam took heed of the warning, but seemed to minimize it initially. "So..." Sam replied thoughtfully. "I'm up here with... who? The Pope? *(No, he woulda went straight up)."* He thought. How 'bout Elvis?" Sam rambled on as he always did when he was getting nervous.

"Doc, what about the other religions? What about the Jews, Buddhists, Baptists, Muslims, Scientologists and so on? All they have to do is repent and/or believe in Jesus and we hang out at the Semi-Heavenly slash Semi-Purgatory mall together?"

Shaking his head at Sam's apparent lack of seriousness, Chuck couldn't help but break out a smile. Knowing all too well Sam's reaction to nervousness, the doctor replied, "Seriously, Sam listen to what I'm saying. I've only been here a little while myself. It can take thousands of years to have even a basic misunderstanding of Heaven and God. All I know is what I've been told. Sam, you're here because you *largely* kept your nose clean."

"*That was an extremely odd thing to say,*" Sam thought; "*Very odd and REAL damned familiar. Who are you.....*"

"Keep that going here and you have a decent shot of going through the metaphysical "pearly gates".... eventually. *If*, that's what *you* want. Here... look..." As the doctor spoke, he moved his hands in a box-like fashion. Instantly, actual blue and cloudy dotted lines appeared in mid air.

Within the lines, a cartoonish set of scripts appeared. They dazzled Sam in brilliant purplish red hues. The play unfolded within the floating box right in front of his eyes. It was a figure on a cross; screaming winds, shaking Earth, complete sadness. The figure looked up one last time. Sam was completely mesmerized. As the play continued, the doctor spoke.

"Take for example, Jesus himself. He lived as a human and died a horrible death. God allowed this to happen to his son not only to make true the prophesies, but so that Jesus would know first-hand the human experience. Although he is both human and divine, only by actual human experience could he be knowledgeable enough to be allowed to pass judgment on those who believe in him."

And with a wave of his hand, it all shimmered away. Sam couldn't believe his eyes. His mouth hung wide open. The doctor went on as if not even seeing Sam anymore. The doctor knew this would "floor" Sam, but he went on smugly as though nothing had just happened.

"However, and this is a big however, there are other religions who are equally as valid. Consider, for example, Muslims. They also have a savior. If they believe in his peaceful works as dictated by the Qur'an and have lived a life that has taught them lessons, then they too are admitted into Heaven or Purgatory.

It kinda comes down to this Sam. For man, almost nothing is possible. For God, everything is possible…Ok?

So it isn't a case of just how you lived by the rules you were taught… although that does count. You also have to believe in God. Ultimately, only through God's grace can one gain Heavenly access. For non believers, they are given a chance to believe here in Purgatory. The rest is up to them."

Sam was nodding and absent mindedly taking it all in, but he was still floored from the visual display. He started to swing his legs off of the bed in a life-long reflex to get up for the day.

"Wait! I know you're anxious". The doctor cautioned.

"But you need to know the ground rules here before going out that door. Purgatory is a plane of existence that a soul is sent to that is just out of Heaven's reach and just out of Hell's. Call it Earth 2.0." The doctor laughed at his own joke.

"I've heard that one before." Sam thought to himself. He couldn't quite make out that laugh….

The doctor continued with the air of a professional. "Purgatory is a realm where souls take on human form, but they are also fully aware of both God's presence. Though we cannot "see" God directly, we do see his Angels continued presence. And if you see God's Angels, well then the opposite is also true, correct? So be careful.

"So I didn't rate Heaven, huh doc? No problem. What can posssssibly go wrong?" Sam chuckled in amusement.

The doctor stopped and for the first time looked at Sam sternly. "Think of your life Sam; *really* think. Think of what You think you deserve. Should you be in Heaven?" As he spoke, the doctor rested his hand slightly on Sam's shoulder.

Instantly, Sam had visibly clear recollections of his past. No… cloudiness, no questions of validity, but real "visions" of his past. He continued to marvel on this new reality. Focusing on the doctor's negative suggestions, the memories came crashing back. He thought of the hurt that he'd caused and viewed them in real time. Desperate gestures of hurt, hope and loss-- The trust that he had betrayed.

"These memories are so real-- Almost *alive.*"Sam whispered. "So clear."

"Yeah, like before all the alcohol, time and age had dampened them." The doctor replied.

Time seemed to drift very slowly and now vibrant colors were now associated with the memories; the same colors as the streams that surrounded him in the tunnel. He could even smell her perfume. He could feel her skin. The tears welled up for the first time as he looked directly into her all too real eyes.

The doctor took off his hand and stopped him quickly. "Whoa partner." He gently infused. "That must've been a deeply sad memory to get through right now. Look, that's enough bad stuff for one day."

Sam noticed that the room had become… darker. "*Odd*" Sam thought somberly.

"Ok, let's try this again. Try to think… happier… thoughts now...." As he spoke, the doctor once again rested his hand on Sam's shoulder. This time, his mind raced back to a beautiful snowy day in Ohio. It brought him directly to his daughter; her glowing face and those awkwardly smiling braces. It was a beautiful day of sledding with her and her Grandpa.

"C'mon Dad, one last time!" she sang. The snow was so very white, the weather crisp, the ice brilliantly shining; Absolute happiness and love that came with it-- a perfect memory.

Sam knew that of all the things that he was (and was not) at least he felt that he'd always tried to be a good Dad. He'd tried to be in his daughter's life every day and was sure that his continued presence within his daughter life was indeed God's grace.

He truly felt that he was allowed to be present in her life not only to guide her, but to work on his own soul as well. It was as if he was able to find self worth in her eyes, if not in his own.

As he pushed her down the hill, the sled gained speed quickly. The old, wooden platform felt hard and unforgiving. This was his sled as a child and his father's before him. Slicing into the snow, the speed increased incredibly.

Oblivious to the danger, she sat safely in front of him in protective cocoon of her dad's legs. Her laughter was unforgettable. He could actually feel the cold as he swam in the memories. Then, in a flash, he saw the icy tree root out of the corner of his eye. At the last second he tried to steer the old sled with his feet-- too late.

They both went up in the air, she with the sled and him on his back. He looked up to see the sun shining through the snow covered limbs of the great oak. "Shit." He said as he sat up dazedly.

He watched helplessly as she went careening down the path; completely safe and laughing hysterically as she did.

Of course, Grandpa was there to stop the old sled at the bottom. It was a perfect day. The vision ended abruptly as the doctor removed his hand. "There, that's better." Doc affirmed. As Sam looked up at the hospital room ceiling, he noticed a slight snow fall had begun…In the room.

"Doc, it's friggin' snowing in here. In the friggin' room."

"Oh yeah, that. Well, that's one of the benefits and downfalls of the afterlife. Our memories are no longer inhibited by our aging minds. And our thoughts can become….physical, but only if they are deep enough. But remember Sam, everything in your previous life has been…. recorded-- everything."

The doc took a second to let this sink in. "*EVERYTHING.*" The doc whispered.

Their eyes met. Immediately the shame came back for his sins-- the transgressions for his actions-- The ripples of his sins.

"Ok, you get my drift. Both the good *and* the bad will come back. So let's stop for now. It's good to remember the past, but it is incredibly bad to relive it often. Take those memories and temper them with the fact that we humans are nothing more than animals. Those animals are then given self awareness, souls and are taught to discern between good and evil. Hell, we were even given lessons and guides on how to live. The problem is that our animal instincts are almost completely contrary to the rules we've been given. Suffice it to say, very few people go directly up."

As the doctor spoke, he again drew a box in the air with his fingers. Cloudy blue dotted lines appeared and within the box a play formed. Two human figures stood in a beautiful landscape; both naked and happy. As the doctor moved his hands behind the box ,the figures moved. The play now started.

The naked male and female were walking in the woods, he laid down to rest, but the woman kept exploring. A large snake appeared and a golden apple was eaten off of a dark green tree. A huge storm bellowed a voice that betrayed an all too familiar story. The look of fear on their faces was familiar….it was shame.

He began to understand that his shame was not alone. That he, was NOT alone. And with a snap of the doctor's fingers, the vision was gone.

"That's really cool." Sam proclaimed. "How'd you do that?" Smugly ignoring Sam and shrugging his shoulders, the doctor continued.

"Shut up and listen. So, we are given a divine choice: Let the animal instincts rule our lives or let our spiritual guidance rule the animal. Heaven is the spirit winning and leaving the body behind. Hell is the body winning and leaving the spirit behind. Purgatory or "Midtown" (as we call it) is….. well…. the in-between. It's really up to you now." Sam nodded slowly.

"That leads to us. That is where you and I are now-- Midtown."

"Midtown?" Sam asked innocently.

But the doctor just went on. "We are the souls that are fully aware of our Earthly deaths and of our new lives here. We live in a world…. Similar…. in nature to Earth and for thousands of years we have built cities and different cultures based on our Earthly beliefs. But there are no deaths or diseases here. Also, churches, synagogues and mosques are here as well. In them you can actually see God's Angels.

So when different faiths believe that praying for the souls of their departed one's help them gain access to Heaven-- it is true. God hears these prayers and combines them with their deeds in Purgatory. If the soul in question is "washed" enough via this combination, they are ultimately granted Heavenly access. The same is true for other religions that pray for their departed. It is a strong combination that through God's grace allows access to Heaven at the lowest level.

Sam, reaching Heaven is all about self-realization. In Heaven, you internalize that you no longer need Earthly things. Ya' know, bodies, sex, money, etc. If you fully believe this, well, up you go. But that's also the problem. Some folks don't want to let go, so they will live their entire afterlives here."

"This is a lot to take in doc." Sam threw up his hands.

"I know." The doctor replied laughingly. "Just know that there are no absolutes here. No defined linear levels, just a level of needs based on spiritual enlightenment. Keep it human and stay here forever as a human. But seek further enlightenment and well……"

"Fine. Look…Ok, Ok, so what's next?" Sam asked with a deep sense of confusion.

"Well, again, that's kinda up to you". The doctor replied. "You can ask to meet your dead relatives, friends, Elvis, other famous people and so on. But be aware that some of them are in Heaven. And in Heaven, they are enjoying the complete absence of crime, hunger and so on. So they can be difficult to understand and since they are in God's presence, it is even hard to actually view them for long periods of time.

You see, when you actually reach Heaven you are no longer in need of your previous human shell. "*For they will be like the Angels*." The doctor looked up and quoted. They will recognize you and love you, but they will have left all of their worldly problems behind. I mean, what do you talk about?"

The doctor took a second and leaned in as if telling a secret. "But I do know a little: They can have similar lives as we do here, but they actually spend most of their time basking in "his glory." The doctor made the international sign for quotations with his fingers and went on.

"You see, "his glory" actually means an aura of pure, absolute love. And once you have experienced perfect love and live in it constantly; well, everything else is kind of a letdown. So again, folks in Heaven get a little… tough to talk to. They just don't understand us anymore, nor we, them. Oh sure, you can actually talk to them and vice versa, but they really no longer understand our lives either."

Sensing that he was completely saturating Sam, he changed the subject and leaned back. "But there's lots of folks to meet right here as well! And some of them *want to* stay here forever. They can and will live their eternity in Purgatory. Not a bad life…umm…death really, but they will never actually know complete happiness. Their happiness will forever be tied to their Earthly needs."

The doctor finished his practiced speech with a sense of seriousness. "Sam, it's a trade off really. Do you want to leave the daily routine behind for limitless joy? Or is your limitless joy in your earthly needs? I mean, it's your after life—you decide."

Confused, but with a renewed sense of strength, Sam replied, "OK doc, enough. I mean, where do I live? I mean, sleep, food...Do I even need all that now?"

"Sort of." The doctor went on to explain. "Let's look at Midtown functionally."

As he spoke, a sly look of humor overtook him. A professor's cap now tilted sideways on his head.

"Where the Hell did that cap come from?" Sam blurted.

Chapter Four

O' Lord… Where am I?

"Quiet dummy." The doctor replied. "So listen up. As you are in a form of Purgatory, you cannot simply manufacture any environment you want. You have already subconsciously manufactured your home and all this landscape around you. This is your well deserved sanctuary. This was all built by God.

So when you look up, you'll see the sun. At night you'll see the moon and the stars and so on. When you're hungry, you eat, etc. Bathrooms and showers are there, but not needed. You see, since you're not actually digesting the food you're eating, there is no need for it. Where's it go? God knows….. But it sure makes plumbing easier." He winked with a smile.

"You'll also have "limited" control of your environment. Rain will come and go as your subconscious recommends and so on. But when you want to go somewhere else… Say, the city of Midtown or to see relatives and so on, you go through a portal of your choosing. You see, we all make our own portals…."

As he spoke, the doctor looked out the window. "Ok, where's your…." As they both looked out the window of the absurdly white hospital room, Sam admired the stately driveway lined with grand Oaks. *"A perfect fall day."* Sam thought *"Leaves bursting all around; An actual bubbling brook; Incredible…"*

"When can I go out there doc?" Sam asked with a smile.

"One second." The doctor warned, "We should find your portal first. Oh yeah, we also need to talk about your home. You see, when you leave this room, it will be gone. Whatever home you have built for yourself will be in whatever landscape you… um, decided. But when you leave the comfort of your own private sanctuary, then you then go into the "collective" Midtown. Get it?"

"Yep. Wait. What? No. Not really." Sam both nodded and shook his head with a sense of humor. The doctor glanced over and smiled, but continued looking out the window.

"Ok, let's take this one step at a time. Let's walk outside before we run to meet others in town…" But as the doctor droned on, clearly he was trying to find something outside.

"Aha!" He proclaimed. "Once we go through that *beautiful* red brick ten foot high gate over there (*nice ivy by the way*) you will see the rest of Midtown. And remember: Midtown is a civilization that is a mix of ancient and modern worlds. A place where limited technology exists, but so does crime."

"Crime"? Sam asked. A genuine look of surprise showing on his face.

"Yes crime; Although it *is* rare." The doctor replied. He sensed the concern in Sam's voice. "Look Sam, Midtown exists because of God. But it is populated and built by man. Man is flawed, so therefore, Midtown is flawed. Midtown exists so that a flawed man can become "clean" enough to ultimately enter Heaven or screw up enough to go, well, *the other way*.

However, crime is pretty much futile here as the offenders are always caught (usually by an Angel) and the offender is always given many chances to repent. But some just reject these chances. You see, some habits are hard to break, even here.

And that's another thing you should know: When you enter the churches, synagogues, temples, and so on, you will notice a figure somewhere near the altar. That shimmering, bright, beautiful being is a no-kidding Angel; The physical manifestation of a spirit class completely subservient to God himself. The Priests, Rabbis, Imams, Reverends and other holy men and women are also still here as spiritual guides themselves.

Some of them are so dedicated that they have actually come back down from Heaven to populate these churches, but some are still working their way up. For those that go back and forth, this is their Heaven-- helping others. But they can go back and forth as they see fit. They can actually be multiple places at once. Do not ask me to explain that one.

But as I said before, those who actually go to Heaven live entirely different lives from those of us here. They live in absolute spiritual bliss, with no need of their human bodies. Think of Heaven as that shiver that goes down your back when something great is happening."

The doctor took a second to think. "I know… remember when the Star Spangled banner played and you'd get that shiver down your back? Well, imagine living that way permanently; absolute joy-- that zeal is Heaven.

But even in Heaven you still have free will. And there are higher callings there as well. You can help those in Purgatory, *try* to help those in Hell, etc… For us here in Midtown, Earth is a very big deal. "Earth?" Sam asked. "I can go home?"

The doctor softened his practiced speech, he could sense the pain in Sam's voice. "Kind of, but not in the way you think. You see, Earth is one great way to continue "washing your soul." You can do this by helping to guide those souls on Earth. But it will never be your own family. You will be allowed to look in on them, I promise. But let's focus on the immediate task ahead, ok?

Look, you can help on Earth or you can refine yourself through good works here. If your thinking guardian Angel, that's about right. Guardian Angels cannot influence directly, but they can…..lean… a person to use their own good judgment." Sam was taking it all in carefully. He had a sense that this was a time to pay attention, but he was thinking of home—of his family. He started to let his mind wander, but the doctor caught him.

Sternly, the doctor cleared his throat. He put up his fingers and started counting. "Sam, this is important. If you want to go up, a few things can happen: One, you do good deeds in Midtown. Two, you help on Earth. Three, you pray for others and/or four; you are prayed for. On Earth, you help by becoming a guardian Angel. Here, by becoming spiritual guides to new arrivals. All of this stuff combined equates to the "cleansing" of your soul. Ok?"

Sam's look was far from Ok.

Ok. So that's what I did; I lived my Earthly life and I volunteered to guide souls (like you), up. And I am ever so slowly, but diligently, working to try to get upstairs." He gave Sam a little bit of a wink at that. He was trying to bring up Sam's unhappiness.

"Slowwwwly trying to get upstairs." The doctor emphasized with a smile. "But diligently." He said as he glanced upwards.

"Look doc. No mas." Sam smiled an unhappy smile. "When can I get outta here and look in on my family?"

"Soon" the doctor replied. But the wound to their spirit is still too fresh." You'll get to see them soon, but when you *all* are ready for it."

Sam thought this over soberly for a second then asked, "OK, well, when can I see God?"

"Of course." The doctor replied thoughtfully. "I'm sorry, but you are not yet ready to be even "able" to see him. As a matter of fact, neither am I. Our souls aren't "pure" enough yet. We can only view him if and when we are "washed enough" to make it through the pearly gates.

But even though you can't view him physically from here, you can view his Angels, those folks are everywhere. Not only will they will be in every place of worship, but they also live among us in Midtown. They're...... undercover... if you will. Sneaky buggers actually, always keeping an eye on things." The doctor winked again.

"You can also "feel" them when they are close. Again that... shiver.... of absolute joy. That feeling is one of the main reasons that souls want to move up from Purgatory to Heaven's levels.

Being in close proximity to the Angels is an extension of being close to God. And being close to God is being close to pure, holy and absolute love. That joy is absolute.

So your direct involvement with God and his Angels will be limited only by your advancement here as your soul will need to be cleansed in able to withstand absolute happiness. As you further cleanse your soul here, it can further withstand God's absolute love. That refinement is done right here."

"Doc, all this time I thought I just kinda floated around like a gumball or maybe played the harp in the clouds." Sam felt like a child in class again. He wanted to be happy, so he tried.

"Well," the doctor mused back. "You are more than welcome to do that. But it seems kinda boring to me." He laughed as he pulled out a flask and took a drink.....

"Alcohol?" he asked. "Yep, VO whisky is quite literally is a friend of mine up here. The doctor replied. As are great softball games!"

"*Things are starting to look up.*" Sam thought.

Catching the mischief in Sam's eyes, the doctor warned: "Remember Sam, my version of Midtown allows alcohol. I just have to be aware of the ramifications of my actions under alcohol's influence. I can still sin here. I can still be forgiven here. But enough of the same sins will move me further from God's grace, aka, down the spiritual levels. Enough of the same and you are given a glimpse of Hell. Usually, those souls that go back that low, get scared enough to stop. I hear there's nothing quite like actually seeing Hell to get your head on right." The doctor knew he was scaring him now. "Look- Wanna meet some dead relatives?" he asked light-heartedly.

"Yeah..." Sam half replied "But what about my daughter?" Sam again felt the pangs of hurt and anger. "When can I at least see her?"

"You could soon." The doctor replied cautiously. "But time happens slightly differently here then it happens on Earth. You've passed only a few weeks there. You, however, have been "rested" here, so that your soul can adjust *and* so that you cannot view your own funeral.

"Sam." The doctor spoke with concern. "Your family is very sad now. But you can visit them soon, I promise. But Sam, when you are "allowed" to see them, don't get too close, ok? If you try to touch or contact them directly, you will actually "touch" their souls. This feeling causes intense sadness to them as it is not natural. You should not view them until time has allowed them to withstand your close proximity to them.

Also, the transition back to Earth is guided by an Angel. If the Angel does not think it's an appropriate time for you to view them, it will not happen.

Privacy and respect for the human overrides your needs. Remember, humans are made in God's image."

Sam looked down. Tears wanted to form. But he just couldn't be sad enough. *"Odd"* he thought.

"Sam. You will see them very soon. I promise, ok?"

At the promise, Sam smiled. He didn't know who this doctor was, but he suspected he wasn't a real "doctor" at all. This guy actually seemed to care—a lot. Way more than any doctor Sam had ever met. He started to feel better and smiled his first genuine smile.

"Ok." The doctor said sympathetically. "Enough of the afterlife 101 stuff, ok? Let's get you walking outside. Can you get up yet?" Trying, Sam almost fell face flat. "Trying to get your sea legs?" The doctor teased.

The doctor bellowed a deep bellowing laugh that again betrayed something-- It was a *family* laugh. All the men in his family had that same damned laugh. It was an innate capability to take the same joke, retell it thirty times and STILL find it funny. The laugh hit Sam like a ton of bricks.

"Grandpa?"

The doctor's eyes widened with recognition. A broad smile crept on his face and his arms opened instantly. He hugged Sam and held him all the while laughing. "Oh my God!" Sam muttered.

"Exactly." Sam's Grandpa responded. "The old man delivers old "Chuck" to your doorstep. And yes, you can call me Chuck your-- call. You are an extremely lucky lad to be in my presence" Chuck proclaimed. Their hug was one for the books.

Chuck forced a split. His eyes welling with the same tears that Sam had "Look damn you, let's not get all mamby-pamby, wishy-washy! Take a look in the damned closet. You'll have your kind of clothes from your life." Sam did as directed.

Sam's mind immediately began swirling with memories of his grandfather; Wonderfully crisp, fall nights, when his Dad, brother and Grandpa would go to the high school football games. What great times those were. "Oh no. he muttered "Mom… Dad…. our family."

"I know" Chuck stated flatly. "But you and I will see them again. This will be hardest on your parents. They wanted so badly to die before their children did- just like you. It's a very unnatural thing"

"I understand grandpa. But it all still sucks."

"Yeah". Chuck admitted. "It does. But like all things in eternity, the only constant is change. Even here; no, especially here, life goes on. Sam stopped and just stared at him. He just couldn't believe that all this was happening.

He looked in the closet and found his favorite pair of jeans, old brown leather boots, underwear, socks and a Mickey Mouse t-shirt. It was a gift from his daughter after Disney.

He felt for his wallet and cell phone but they weren't there. "Of course" he thought—this will take some getting used to. As he stepped behind the divider to change, he wondered aloud as he saw a shelf with toiletries. "Do I need deodorant?" The sound of the question itself smacked with absurdity.

Chuck laughed loudly. "No. Right now, your body "seems" as real here as it was there. But you won't age unless you want to. You'll also "want" food, toiletries, the toilet, and so on.

Sam slipped on his clothes and noticed the well fit 34/34 jeans were a little loose. "Ha! I guess I finally lost those ten pounds after all!" He peered over the divider to see his Grandpa smirking. His white lab coat was now next to him on the table.

Chuck wore a long sleeved, light tan, cotton work shirt rolled to the elbows. Light blue suspenders, brown slacks and a taxi cab driver's hat made him look like a construction worker straight out of the depression. It was so odd to see the old man this fit.

"This must have been what he looked like before the years had racked his body." Sam thought to himself.

Walking toward Sam, he could see that the metal rod from the cancer in his leg was no longer there. The smile that was on Chuck's face was there so much more now than during his life on Earth. Sam also noticed that Chuck quickly reached down onto the night stand next to the bed and slid what looked like a book into his back pocket.

The well worn, rolled up white paperback was embossed with golden writing. He jammed into his back pocket. Sam could just make out a portion of the golden lettered title "The Mi…"

"Ready to go?" Chuck said. As he spoke, he put a wad of chewing tobacco in his mouth.

Sam just smiled.

Chapter Five

And Let the Rocket 88 Roll

It didn't take long for Sam to get his "sea legs" going. When they left the hospital room, they stepped into a plush green landscape that took both of them by surprise. The immediate lawn was Ohio green, but the landscape far off to the west was all North Carolina Blue Ridge. Off to the east was an absolutely clear and pristine ocean. The sand of the beach was a mix of white and turquoise. On the other side of the ocean he could see more mountains and an adobe red desert. It seemed to go on forever.

"Beautiful." Sam remarked.

"Yeah." Chuck said, "rebuilt from the best of your past." As Sam turned around, where had once been a hospital room was now an old southern plantation. A nice mid size Antebellum house with wrap-around porch and three car garage. The house was beautiful, but he thought it was a bit much. He had little need for such Earthly dwellings, even on Earth. He just tried to keep up with what he was given.

That was something he'd always believed in; You made your own luck by working hard, but ultimately he knew that God giveth and God taketh away. He'd learned those lessons during his not one, not two, but three war tours.

"A Garage?" Sam blurted out in astonishment.

"Hey, it's your little slice of almost Heaven", Chuck replied. "But I'll be I know what's inside." Sam wanted to sprint to open the doors, but oddly enough walking was still taking a little getting used to. He just felt…lighter.

Sam looked at his Grandfather as they reached the garage door. "Go ahead" Chuck said. Sam rolled up the door to see what he knew was already there. It was the family 1958 Oldsmobile Rocket 88.

Her chrome gleamed brilliantly. She was clean right down to the fire engine red top and Alaskan white body. Sam noted with pride that she had just a little too much chrome for her own good.

"I'll bet the damned thing is still a bitch to start." Sam joked.

"Well, it better not be. I got a little tired of the prayers for help when you were down there." They both laughed aloud-- that familiar family chuckle.

"Let's take her to town!" Sam blurted.

"Wait, where's your riding partners?" Chuck asked. At that, Sam spun around to the sound of not one dog barking, but two… *"Dogs?"* Sam thought. *"What the…."* To his amazement, from around the house, ran Sugar and Rags. They were Sam's basset hound and long haired sheep dog that he had as a child. They were both amazingly spry and jumped on him as soon as they saw him.

Tumbling to the ground, Sam laughed lovingly. Both dogs were vying for attention and licking his face. "Whoa!" Sam laughed. "How you guys been????" Both dogs sat and looking at him lovingly.

"Tell ya what." Chuck said. "We got all eternity to play. You two mutts go on inside and we'll play later." Chuck commanded "Inside!" But both dogs just looked at him sideways, like all dogs do when they're confused.

Sam, reading the situation, commanded "Home!" and both dogs scurried into the side door. *"Of course the side door had a dog door…. of course."* Sam laughed to himself and shook his head.

"Figures." Chuck said in resignation. "Those mutts know you all too well. You know, seeing as how dead dogs knock you down and you still walk a little weird, it *may* be a good idea for us to *walk* to town rather than drive. You're literally still learning to walk here. Operating a heavy vehicle may not be the best option." Chuck teased.

"Good idea." Sam sheepishly responded. "I won't even think about the motorcycle next to it. "But what's the third spot for?" he asked confusedly.

"Knowing you, it will be some sort of fighter airplane or somethin'. You better find a flight instructor in town before conjuring up that baby; Maybe your Grandpa Ken from WWII?" Chuck asked seriously.

"Really?" Sam asked.

"Really." Chuck responded.

"*This was going to be very interesting indeed.*" Sam thought. "OK, Good deal. Do we take the driveway? It seems a bit long" Sam asked.

"Or the gate through the high brick fence there." Chuck responded. We just open the wrought iron and walk through. They walked down the red brick sidewalk and approached the gate. It seemed to pulse with life and emanated a slight warmth. Sam noted with interest that he couldn't quite see through the iron. Only that vague figures shimmered behind it.

"Ummmm. I'm not so sure." Sam looked at Chuck with wide eyes.

Ignoring him with a resigned smirk, Chuck opened the gate. He stepped through the ripples and only left one arm and hand behind through the pulse.

"C'mon."

"Shit." As Sam left his sanctuary, a slight wind blew and the smell of roses and cinnamon filled the air. "Odd." He thought. "I don't see any rosebushes." As he took his first step, he felt with one foot very… slowly…. forward. It took only bringing in the second foot and he was there. But that second step seemed to take forever. He looked up to see an amazing sight.

There they were, standing on an emerald green hill side overlooking a city of immense size. Beautiful Victorian buildings cloistered next to medieval castles, next to Arabic domes, next to Jewish temples, next Christian churches and so on. Asian temples and Hindu palaces also filled every crevice.

The colors of the buildings were as varied and vibrant as the people who drifted there. He could smell the jasmine, the cooking beef, the fresh cut grass; the sounds and smells of life. "Amazing." Sam muttered to himself.

"Yeah. It's really something to see the first time, isn't it?" Chuck responded with practiced empathy. "Look over there, over in the sandy area."

Off to the side, Sam saw what seemed to be an actual set of Saharan huts made of hides. Mountains also rose to the West and a vastness of water lay to the North. A vast Desert sat to the South and behind was him open field of emerald hills. His gate was sitting atop one of the hills.

A mix of people walked to and fro. They were in everything from Victorian dress to business suits to togas and shorts. Everyone was milling about, making small talk and enjoying the day.

They started to walk and Sam froze. "Grandpa." Sam whispered, "what is that?

Confused, Chuck looked up, searched and saw it. "Oh, that is an Angel flying."

"WHAT?!" Sam replied almost screaming. "Yep. See 'em all the time. So watch your P's and Q's." Chuck smiled and walked forward.

Floored, Sam walked quickly to catch up. Taking a second to think, Sam blurted, "Lemme guess. Seeing as how there's only a few gates and hills, that gate over there is not only for my home, but can get other folks home too Right?" Chuck opened his eyes wide with feigned astonishment. "Very good. Your getting the hang of this."

As they continued their walk, Sam noticed a series of underground tunnel openings also dotted the landscape. From them proceeded a myriad of cars, trucks, motorcycles, horses, buggies and trolleys *"but no electrical lines"* Sam thought. "And parking?" Sam asked. "Yep," Chuck responded. "LOTS of it-- Everyone loves their rides, including the Amish."

"Yeah, remember when Dad took us to that place with five hundred cheeses?" They both roared again. *"I missed that laugh."* Sam mused.

They walked further down the hill next to a twisting red brick road coming from his wrought iron fence. The brick was dotted with signs of fresh grass sprouting through the cracks.

"How do they mow all this?" Sam thought to himself. The grass was all so even, so…. perfect. "Grandpa, how do we actually get home?" Sam asked. "Will we be able to see it once were in the city?"

"It will always be within sight. Don't try to make me explain that one". Chuck for the first time shrugged in confusion.

"Fair enough," Sam said. "*So, the old….um….young…. man wasn't omnipotent after all. Thank God!*" As they walked, Sam noticed that the streets were all lit with gas lamps. The buildings also only had fire. "I thought you said there was technology here?" he said.

"Limited technology." Chuck replied. "In Midtown itself you'll find no firearms (gunpowder doesn't light here), no computers and no electric. Same goes for your home. Oddly enough, there are no telephones either. The refrigerator has ice in it, sitting in a basket. The food you want is always in the drawers, in baskets. But again, I can't explain it….."

The obvious hint on the baskets seem to elude him. Instead of wanting to know where food came from, he wondered instead of…"Wait. No computers? But those things make a lot of…uh… my generation happy." Sam said.

"Yes and no." Chuck replied. "They also led to the greatest trick the Devil ever pulled—"free speech" and the internet. The complete dissemination of some good stuff, but a Hell of a lot more bad stuff." Sam thought that one over. Chuck was right. There was some very creepy stuff out there.

Almost reading his mind again, Chuck spoke like a teacher. "Look, I think it's time to teach ya somethin' else. Do you want the cool learning visual box trick again?"

"No no, I'm good. What's the lesson Socrates….."

Chuck snickered. "Sex."

"Sex?" Sam replied cautiously.

"Yep. It's possible. But you'll notice that your sexual needs in Midtown will be greatly reduced. Your body will be age 20, but your needs will be more like 50. It takes some getting used to and if you want to have sex, you still can. But you really have to want it.

It is odd though, those sexual levels actually increase with actual feelings of love here, Like it probably should have been on Earth. Instead of sex and love being separate, they are very, very linked here. And I wouldn't advise premarital sex too often here, just sayin."

Sam took that in. It was actually a great relief to have that monkey of his back. "So there are marriages here?"

"Oh yeah, it can happen, but not children. Also, divorces can happen here. You see, there are courts here. One of which is actually run by Solomon himself. But divorce here is rare as it is an unhappy event and unhappiness leads to lesser spiritual enlightenment. Remember, a lot of folks here are actually trying to go upstairs. Only some want to live permanent Earthly lives here. Love between people is possible, but the overall focus of most is....well...upwards.

You just have to remember the power of God's love here. It overshadows human love like an ocean to a river. Once you feel (like you have) absolute love. You focus on attaining more of that than anything else. However, like I said before, some folks shy away from that love and focus on more Earthly needs. Eventually, they leave behind all things spiritual and live a secular life here or..........

"Or what?" Sam asked, but knew.

"Or Hell". Chuck replied flatly. "Hell hath many levels as well. Hell can be many things: From a self imposed stay to escape God's love, to a mandatory punishment for a life desecrated. You, my friend are some where's on the GOOD side of that equation. You have been given a second chance. What will you do with it?"

"*Good question.*" Sam thought. "*What will I do with it? I suppose that there will be no third chance at this....*"

Chapter Six

Perpetual Light and Ari's Place

As they walked down the rolling hillside, the apparent mix of divinity and humanity within the city was both impressive and overwhelming. The buildings were huge and arrayed in a compilation of cultures that were mind boggling. Small European type markets tucked in next to Asian groceries. Jews and Muslims chatted endlessly and walked down the street. Black, White, Indian, it didn't matter. All the peoples of the world just…. Living together.

Sam couldn't comprehend the vastness of it all. "Is that an actual Samurai?" Sam blurted out openly. The Asian man heard him and smirked slightly, but just walked away shaking his head.

"I don't think that's what you call him, but I'd start off with asking him his name." Chuck said softly laughing. "You see, here there are no language barriers; only cultural barriers. Once we learn to overcome them, we can see that we are all not so different after all".

"I'd love to talk to him." Sam replied anxiously.

"We can do that later, but aren't you thirsty or hungry?" Oddly enough, it never occurred to Sam.

"I am slightly hungry."

"And you always will be; hungry… that is. In this way, you'll always be reminded that this is not a perfect world Sam. Eat until your full, drink until your good, but you will always….want…a little something more. I suppose this is God's way of subtly reminding us that this isn't Heaven.

Sam pondered it all as they walked. Chuck knowingly wandered into a nearby bistro. "I love this place" Chuck said with a smile. "Let's grab a beer and a bite."

"Aristotle's Agora" was advertised in red letters on the white shield hanging above the door. The place was a mix of marble ionic columns and flowing purple wall hangings. Yellow lilies were placed on each white concrete table.

A young man in a traditional toga greeted them at the door. "Two?" he asked. Sam was still too much in awe to answer. The young Greek looked at Chuck and said "This him? He looks like he just got here….damned new guys". They both laughed at Sam as they walked to the nearest table. Sam walked slowly behind, not wanting to look any more stupid than he already did.

"Please, please sit" the Greek proclaimed. "As always, drinks are on the house. Chuck, VO or something a little smoother this afternoon? Care for a "*Plate-O-fries*? Get it? Plato fries? Sam is it? Get it new guy? Never mind. I'll be right back. VO?" Chuck just nodded and smirked. Sam sat down completely dumb struck.

"Is that really him? Aristotle?" Sam asked surprised.

"Yep." Chuck replied. "At least you didn't blurt out Samurai this time or somethin'. Look, don't worry 'bout it, he's a good guy. But he's a perfect example of someone who will be here forever; somebody tied to Earthly desires but not deserving of Hell. Overall. that's either happy or sad depending on your viewpoint. Shhh… here he comes."

"Call me Ari, Sam. I gotcha a gyro and pop, cool?" Sam just couldn't believe his ears. Here was one of the founding fathers of modern philosophy speaking in near slang and grabbing food- for him!

"Wait….sir….um…" Sam fumbled for the right words. "Let me guess" Ari responded. "Why the bistro? Why not sit on my pedestal and think deep thoughts?" Sam just nodded in astonishment.

"In all my…..*(what? thousands?)* of years of giving advice I've learned two things. One: Beware Greeks bearing gifts and two: Only the man upstairs truly KNOWS what's going on. The rest of us are just doing the best we can. Here, eat your food". He laid the plate and glass down and leaned over to Chuck "poker tonight?"

"You betcha." Chuck winked in reply. As Ari walked away Sam asked "There's money here?"

"No, no, we play for Reese's Pieces—love them damn things." *"This is just ridiculous"* Sam thought and gave Chuck a look of incredulity.

"That's a good point newbie. No money, no banks, no supermarkets, no infrastructure, etc. What we have here is a society that exists directly on God's benevolence.

I hear that back in the day, there were a few crude buildings here made by the first to be allowed. Then, things kinda took off as more and more souls arrived with more and more knowledge. But you will find that food and everything you need will be given from the baskets like the sermon on the mount deal. See the kitchen there?"

Sam looked over the long counter to see Ari reaching into a series of baskets. "Wait, no way…" Sam uttered.

"Yep. Think of what you want and there it is. The best part is actually the clay pots. Always filled with water or water to wine…" At this, Chuck smirked and looked around, then stopped cold.

For the first time, Sam noticed a male figure sitting in the corner of the room casually looking out of the window. A handsome, almost shimmering, silvery skinned man wearing a dark tunic and carrying a… *(is that a sword?)* Sam thought, dangling on his belt. The man smiled at Sam and for the first time he felt a rush of joy wave through his body; A literal shiver of excitement shoot quickly down his spine. Sam quickly glanced down as the man continued to look out the window.

"What or who is that?" Sam whispered.

"Yep... Angel." Chuck whispered back. "They are everywhere and nowhere. Didja feel the jolt?" Sam nodded in silence.

"Can we talk to him?"

"Well, I think it may be a little much for you. That jolt and love are at a constant when you interact. No way you're ready for that yet, OK? I mean, you should see Angels in their Heavenly splendor—Sam, you can barely even look at them."

Sam just nodded sheepishly and dove into the gyro while keeping an eye on the Angel. "*Damn! I mean darn, this is good.*" Sam thought.

The angel seemed to widen his grin as he gazed out the window.

As Sam finished his lunch, Chuck sipped on his whiskey and tilted the glass in the angel's direction. The angel nodded his head back. "They're not like you and I, you know." Chuck seemed to read Sam's mind. They are here to guide and help refine those of us trying to go upstairs. But talking to them is like talking to a wall.

Oh, they'll be courteous and kind and all, but "small talk" is redundant to them. They are all about the mission: Helping to determine who stays here, who goes up and who goes down."

Sam glanced over at the Angel in awe. "So be careful when interacting with them." Chuck warned. "They are on the streets and in the houses of worship. On the streets, they monitor and enforce. Also, they help to refine."

"What do you mean….refine?" Sam had a hard time calling him Chuck, especially when he felt so very……young and new to all this. "Well Sam, you used to go to church once a week just like before, right?" Chuck asked.

Sam knew this was a vast overestimate. "Sure…Oooo Kayyy. Pretty much…." Sam replied cautiously. He could hear the church lecture coming up.

"*Am I going to have to spend every day in church?*" Sam thought with a slight fear.

Chuck continued, "Well, if *(and this is a big if)* we continue to live better lives here and/or the prayer deal works, then incrementally, we become more and more…refined. This may ultimately lead to us heading upstairs."

"Well that's a good deal, right?" Sam replied happily.

"Umm… yeah, but there's a catch 22". Chuck replied cautiously.

"Go ahead" Sam countered.

"Well, we have no actual indication how or when we are going to be refined. It's not a one- time deal. It's little bits here and there. And I can tell you, it hurts- kinda."

"What?" Sam spoke loudly.

"Yep. Remember that fire during your transition? Well, you get to feel that again." Chuck relied teasingly.

"No way!" Sam blurted. "How can that be?" At the outburst, the angel glanced over. His smile was gone. A very blank look was now on his face.

"Whoa partner-- Don't worry so much." Chuck replied and looked at him with merciful eyes. "It's not nearly what you encountered initially. Think of it as little…. hot flashes. The burning of your old sins as your soul becomes more and more pure. Every time we go to church there is the chance of actually receiving this cleansing.

It's actually the Holy Spirit running through you. Burning out the bad and leaving the good. I's also accompanied by the most beautiful music and feeling of absolute tranquility and joy. But the initial "heat" is a bit strong.

I'm told that near the end of our time here, the heat actually becomes an icy, soothing feeling. Don't ask me to explain that one either."

"And we never know when it's gonna happen?" Sam asked.

"Nope." Chuck replied. "I've been here awhile and have gone through many of em. Old Ari over there doesn't even go to church so it will never happen to him. But he knows the deal, maybe one day he'll want more. All we can do is pray for him. But he's gotta want it too, got it?"

"Yeah, but I'm not looking forward to it". Sam replied. Don't worry, you'll be fine." Chuck replied. For the first time Chuck looked at him worryingly. "Just keep your nose clean and work it out."

Smiling, Sam felt that old dynamic in their relationship. That this young man was still his grandfather and was still giving him wise grandfatherly advice. Sam looked over and the Angel was gone.

"Kinda cool how they do that, huh?" Chucked winked and smiled. "Look, let's get outta here and see the sights!"

"Sounds great. Where to? Church?" Sam replied with innocent, but feigned excitement. Sam was weary of the concept of spending every day in church.

Ignoring his sarcasm, Chuck replied. "Well, there's no real map as this place as it is constantly changing. No oversight, no rule of man. Just a collection of.....everything. You see, we don't have to mine to get the raw materials, but we still have to build by hand."

"Lemme guess, the baskets?" Sam smiled.

"Yep, big ones for lumber, oh boy." They both laughed that deep family laugh. It was good to be with him again.

But Chuck also knew what Sam was thinking. That every day was going to be church day. This gave Chuck great delight and Chuck decided to tease him a little. "Is there anything else you want to know about daily life?"

Not wanting to offend anyone and risk the fires below, Sam replied carefully. "Well, I really want to know when I could go to the movies or play Xbox or all the other outlets of my previous life." Then, he really took a chance. "I used to go to church weekly (umm...mostly), but it seems like I should be there daily, right? I mean, I want to go as I'm used to going, but getting zapped....man...."

Chuck let out a laugh that spun heads on the street around. "Look, don't worry buddy, it's not *that* bad. We don't have to live overly pious lives! Just go once a week and be happy, ok? Granted, there's no strip joints, but a lot of other cool stuff is here, so just relax!" Chuck laughed and slapped him on the back.

"OK" Sam replied finally. He felt like a babe in the woods. "So what exactly is in Heaven? It seems like this place is pretty good, so Heaven must be awesome!"

"Well, Heaven is still sort of a mystery to us down here." Chuck replied. All I can tell you is that those in Heaven who come back here do so at their own free will and return more often than they stay here. Up there, they speak of no bodies and absolute love. They almost sing of being everywhere at once and being in HIS presence.

Chuck leaned in close and whispered to Sam, "When anyone is asked specifics, they just kinda.....smile. They all say the same thing. It cannot *be* defined, that it's just too awesome!" As they spoke they could both "feel" an emanating jolt of absolute love and happiness coming from the nearby Angel. Sam never felt better.

As it passed, they both looked at each other. The mystery of what just happened completely mesmerizing them. "Oh, I GOTTA see that!" Sam whispered with the anxiousness of a seven year old boy in his voice.

"Actually, me too." Chuck replied. "Especially since they can go to and from Heaven at will. It's very interesting indeed."

Chuck then sat back. "You know, Grandma went up years ago." He reflected softly as he spoke. "She comes back often to visit me. But she would only smile when I ask her about us being married up there. She only responds that that's not how it works. That the love for and from God outweighs all other Earthly desires. She says she's more of a....completely "happy" soul up there, that there are no "needs" at all. But that she is waiting for me. To tell you the truth, it's difficult for me to fully comprehend."

For the first time since they were together, Sam could see that everything was indeed not perfect in Midtown. He could sense the fragility and needs of someone having problems other than himself. It was almost reassuring and scary at the same time.

After an awkward moment, Sam cleared his throat and spoke up. "Well Grand...., I mean "Chuck", now that I've eaten with Aristotle and have had my mind completely blown, can we *maybe* let me see my family and *maybe* start working on this advancement thing?"

Sam was starting to be truly happy again; a sense of direction and mission once again in his voice. "Well, OK," Chuck replied thoughtfully. "But we need to go back to your gate to make the trip. An angel will be there to guide us. If the situation is right, you will be allowed to view your family. But are you absolutely sure about this Sam? You don't just want to settle in for a while? You sure you need this so soon? "

"I'm sure." Sam replied cautiously. But Sam knew that he was nowhere sure about anything right now.

Chapter Seven

Shine On, Good Intentions…

They walked from the Greek area and back up the hillside to his gate. Along other hills, other souls were doing the same thing. They would walk alone or in pairs and just as they started to walk in, the air around the gate would….smear. They all emanated a wave of colors where the person should be, then…. nothing.

When reaching his gate, Sam peered in to see a ripple in the air that surrounded his house in Midtown. Then, the ripple grew wider. The house slowly transformed into his old house on Earth. The old single story home with the long porch in the front that he and his wife used to enjoy so very often.

"What do I do?" Sam asked Chuck without looking at him with the innocence of a young boy. His eyes transfixed on the home that safely housed his family.

"Well, since you can see your house, so it must be ok to visit, but remember, it's only been a few weeks or so—damn—look, just step on through like before.' Chuck replied. "But I cannot go with you this time. It will only be you and her." Chuck pointed to the left of the house.

Sam noticed a shimmering woman standing on the other side of the portal. Her eyes brilliantly blue and her face held a sympathetic smile. She held out her hand, willing him forward. Grabbing it, he stepped through.

He kept his eyes trained directly on her and held his breath. He felt a cold rush, heard Heavenly music playing, smelled the flowers and then…nothing. He was just standing in his front yard. He was once again completely awed at the experience that just moved him.

Her hand was warm and slight. She looked at him and he looked away, the brilliance of her eyes seemingly looking through him. They dropped hands as she pointed up toward the house. All the while saying nothing but smiling all the same.

Around her body, there was a glowing white where wings on paintings would be. A golden aura softly glowed where a halo should be. Sam was in awe of this woman. The Angel, seemingly reading his mind, just smiled slightly. She pointed to the front door of the house. Her dress was a deep gold that seemed to shimmer with the sun. Overtaken with the situation, Sam could only blurt; "I just GO up?"

Cupping her hand forward to show the way, the Angel only nodded a sympathetic gesture.

"OK" he replied under his voice. His knees shaking as he went up. "*Someone has to mow the lawn.*" He thought.

As he walked up the front wooden stairs, he noticed that the old house still had its charm. It had an inviting swing on one end and a ceiling fan and rockers on the other. And yes, the old wooden front door still needed a coat of paint. He held out his hand to turn the handle. It opened! "W*hat the…I thought I'd be like a ghost!*" Sam thought.

"*Your only thinking that the door opened.*" A female voice said softly in his head. Step through and look behind you. Once more in awe, he immediately did as she said. He closed the door and looked at the lock. Although he never locked it, it was locked none the less.

The angel continued: "*Your reality is similar to her physical reality. But yours never actually happens. Only her world is happening. You gain access by thinking physical differences are happening, but they are not. Also, if there's something that you should not see, I will not allow you to see it.*"

Her sympathetic voice became a little more serious in his head.

"I understand." He lied.

He actually wanted to break down. This was all happening so fast. He was starting to feel the first tears of his new life. On the wall was the picture of his daughter smiling down on him. "*God, I love that picture.*" He thought.

"Where is she?"

The Angel pointed to his daughter's room.

The house smelled of wet dog and stagnant air. As he walked through the house he saw all the old things in life that one comes to love: His daughter's art on the wall, furniture well broken in, that old pot belly stove. All these things seemed so…. unreal now.

He slowly made his way to his daughter's room. The old white wooden door shut as usual. Nobody loves their privacy like a teenage girl does.

He almost broke a smile until he went to push it in. Unsure of himself, he just stood there. "Just push it" The angel spoke, now using her voice openly. Her voice was very calm and very feminine. It seemed to sooth his entire being as she spoke. It reminded him of his mother's voice when he was a child. He missed the bedtime stories that would lull him into the secure sleep of the loved. He also missed reading those same stories to his own daughter.

He put his hand on the door and wanted to push, but for the first time he could hear the sobbing behind the door.

"Can I help her?" Sam asked with tears now in his own eyes.

"No" the Angel responded softly. "Actually, if you get too close to her, she will feel your spirit. This will cause deep despair far worse than she's feeling now."

"Oh God, why…." Sam whispered. His voice starting to crack.

"But how would you know happiness without sadness?" the Angel softly asked.

"She needs to know that I'm OK. She needs to know that I love her." He could barely speak. He was shaking all over.

"You can tell her." she replied. "But the words will be for your own benefit. She will hear nothing. For only time will heal her. God has sent her his spirit, but she is fighting his solace. Sam, you have raised her well; she will feel his grace soon. You know…" she said with hope in her voice, "She cannot *hear* your words, but she can *feel* your intentions."

“I don’t understand.” He weakly offered. Tears were now streaming from his eyes.

He was confused, hurting and began to think that this whole trip seemed like a horrible mistake. Especially hearing his little girl cry. He would do anything to make that stop. He pushed just a little to crack the door. He could see her curled up in a ball at the top of her bed.

She was completely wrapped around his old flannel work jacket. That old, ratty, blue and grey checkered flannel jacket that he wore around the house when he was fixing this or that. “Fiddling around.” His wife used to call it. But with all the sadness, he did take some comfort noticing her loving 80 pound boxer laying at the base of her bed. His tired, large boxer’s was head resting comfortably on her feet. He looked right at him, wagged his tail, turned his head and went to sleep.

“*This is too much.* I’ve made a mistake” Sam thought. “Goodnight. I love you.” He whispered to her. As he spoke, an evening ray of sunshine entered the room. The warm sun gently caressing her tear stained cheek. His daughter smiled ever so mildly. As the ray warmed her, the faint smell of roses drifted in the air. As he turned to leave, he wondered about the sun, the smells, the coincidence of sun and her smile. The Angel smiled pitifully and took a step back. “Want to go back?” She inquired softly.

Sam took a second. “No….. Is my wife here?”

“Yes, she’s in the garden in the back.”

“Ok…. let’s go.” He replied purposefully; false bravado willing him forward. They walked through the small kitchen to the back porch. As he walked down the back stairs he could hear the familiar rush of spraying water on the garden. As he made his way around the bushes he found her there, sitting dazed in the wicker chair. Water and tears ran as free as the hose. She just stared ahead. She just stared.

Sam dared not step closer, remembering the Angel’s warning of closeness. “Damn it, I’m sorry.” He said. Tears were running from both their eyes.

“It will take her a bit longer” The Angel offered. Your death can literally make or break her. She is at her lowest now. So she will either wallow in despair or find…him.” She said quietly and pointed up.

"If you pray for her and guide her, she may just find that relationship. But know that you will never be her guardian Angel. For she may find another to love in this life and if she does, then she deserves her privacy. But you can visit her before that time and sometimes during that time, if it is deemed appropriate. Look, try what you did before" she volunteered.

"What?" Sam said softly, still staring at his wife.

"Use words of your love to comfort her… then watch."

He thought for a second and smiled. "I love you so very much. Be well and feel my love. I will never, ever, ever leave you."

Slowly, the mist from the sprinkler shifted with a slight breeze from the wind. A small rainbow formed over the garden. She looked at it and looked down. She lit up a cigarette and took a pull. A small water droplet landed on the tip and put it out. She blankly looked at the cigarette and then looked at the rainbow. She tamped the cigarette out on the concrete pad below her. She would never smoke again.

"We should go" the Angel said. The process will take a long time and all of you need time and space to begin to heal. But I promise you this, you will see them again."

The wind shifted and the rainbow grew wider. The angel looked at him and smiled. They walked down the sloping green back yard to the forest. His brick gate was there. As he walked through he could hear her getting up and turning off the water. She was getting ready for the day.

"*You go girl.*" Sam thought with a renewed sense of hope. The scent of fresh roses just reached him as he entered the gate to go back.

Chapter Eight

Upon Them, A Promise Of A Rose

He made it back through his gate alone. He had hope in the healing process for his girls, but was not going to see them again for a while. It was just too damned hard. Looking at his new surroundings in Midtown, he had to admit that he admired the large structure that was his house. It was like he'd always dreamed; a complete wrap around front porch, with two wooden rockers. But it was not "home." Home is where your family is. He was hoping to one day have his family back on that porch.

He half heartedly entered and noticed that the inside also had all the usual trappings of life: An oversized couch, rocker, fireplace, etc. It was a beautiful, gilded, cage. In the corner was an old hand started record player like he had seen in the old movies. He ventured further to find a study. It was complete with all of his pictures of life. Including, he marveled, pictures that he couldn't possibly have taken. One photo showed his daughter dancing on the beach. Another, his extended family photo—Everyone was there. The surprising images of his life both left him feeling both elated and sad.

"Another shortfall of this new life I suppose. Not quite Heaven, but way far from Hell. If I stay in this limbo, I suppose I'll always be left…. wanting. Damn. " He whispered.

He wandered into the kitchen to find a large ice box like he saw in pictures from during the depression. In it, he found a series of cold, wicker baskets. The large one on top contained ice and was incredibly cold. He opened a random brown basket below to find nothing there.

Shaking his head, he thought he must be doing something wrong.

"*Oh yeah. Think….* "He closed the basket and thought again. This time, he thought of salty bacon and fresh eggs. He then opened the basket to find a beautiful half slab of almost fat free bacon with a half dozen eggs.

"*Amazing. Perhaps this won't be so bad after all.*"

He found some matches in the basket and lit the antique gas stove and found the coffee basket. He started to smile, but threw down the coffee in frustration.

"I'm not ready to be alone. I wish Grandpa was here."

Frying the bacon, he heard a bell ringing by the gate outside. He looked in the direction of the noise to see the gate faintly pulsing on the fence. The dogs bounded from the kitchen door, barking wildly and stopping just short of the gate. The little chime bell just continued to ring its soft chime.

Not knowing what to do, Sam just muttered "Uh, come in?" and threw his hands up in frustration. Instantly, Chuck came strolling through the front door, suntan lotion, chair and bathing suit on. He wore an obnoxious white sun block stain on his nose. The whole sight was as ridiculous as Sam's new situation was.

"What the…" Sam blurted with a smile. Chuck cut him off with a wave of his hand.

"Whenever you want anyone, just think of them. Then you have to invite them over. I get the invite on a letter in a basket in my mailbox, complete with a ringing chime. If I *want* to come over, I walk next door to your gate (and yes, we "all" live next door to each other). I ring the bell and you answer and "Voila!" He went on to courtesy with feigned respect.

Sam's smile rapidly erased. "Grandpa, I'm not sure I'm ready to be alone." he said flatly.

"Ahhhhhh, a case of post-mordem stress. It happens to the best of us. It's tough seeing the fam, huh?"

"Yeah." Sam replied.

Sensing that he misjudged the seriousness of the situation, Chuck lowered his humorous tone and spoke with sincerity. "Ok, let's get you outta here. Look, there's an endless list of things we can do. There's daily life, or a more…. adventurous and esoteric life."

"What do you mean?" Sam perked up.

"Well, basically, we can go on an adventure to another time and slash or place. You pick it, we walk through your gate and "Bam!" we're in it." Chuck replied.

"No kidding?" Sam asked incredulously.

"No kidding. You pick it. What's your fancy?" Chuck replied.

Sam had to think that one through. He loved the medieval period, but that seemed....aggressive.... for his first trip into whatever this was. The old history buff in him came out. "Well, what about American history? Maybe the Revolutionary war?" Sam asked.

"Done. Now we go to your closet, pick out the appropriate outfits and step on through. I gotta tell ya though; You can kill or be killed. At which time, you will once again wake up in that awful hospital bed.

Also, pain is very real and you are never truly out of *his* sight, so remember that your actions in these "alternative realities" are recorded. These...adventures.... are just further ways to refine your soul. But they can also be further ways to darken it—remember that." Chuck warned firmly.

"Understood." Sam replied almost militaristically. The excitement of the idea was beginning to hit home. "This will be a much needed diversion Grandpa." Sam noted softly. "Let's get outta here."

As they walked upstairs to Sam's bedroom, he opened his closet to find a complete set of uniforms and ranks from the Revolutionary war.

"What'll it be? North or South?" Chuck asked slyly. It took Sam a second—"Wait, what???

"Just kidding-- keepin' you on your toes." Chuck teased. "Ha! Here's a good one: Let's both be Polish infantry. They were sent to the Gulf in the first Gulf War and Mexico didn't know what to do with them! Get it?"

They both laughed the deep, obnoxious family laugh.

"Remember grandson, only people of true Polish descent can tell Polish jokes. Everyone else is just a wanna be!"

"*It's good to be together again.*" Sam thought.

As they put on their uniforms, they found swords, muskets with bayonets on the floor. "You sure you wanna do this?" Chuck asked.

"Look, we won't even shoot." Sam replied. "I just want to take a look around and see what's what, Ok? But how do we get in and out? An Angel? The gate?"

"You guessed it." Chuck replied. We go through the gate to somewhere it puts us. Also, all the other people in the other dimension will be unaware of our….beginnings. We will be going to their reality, but we won't belong there. Also, there may be a mix of other Midtowners like us.

We won't know one from the other. It's kinda neat actually." Chuck took a second to let it sink in. "Ok Sam, it's a plan. We take the trip and get out at the first sign of real danger, good?" Chuck asked. Sam just nodded.

"I gotta tell ya, I'm a little wary of your plan. My first adventure was going back to a Cleveland Browns game from the 1960's. So when we want out, one of us just thinks of the gate, ok?

It will show in a very off the way location. We high tail it through and get home, deal?" Chuck seemed even more cautious in his approach.

"Deal!" Sam replied anxiously. "Let's hit the road!"Chuck just looked up and offered a feigned prayer "The Lord loves drunks and fools, seems like we got the market cornered."

Sam knew he'd heard that before. "C'mon Old man" Sam chuckled in agreement.

As they stood in front of the mirror, they couldn't help but smile at the awkwardness of it all. Two blue coats with white canteens and black leather boots. Perfect and clean in appearance, they knew they would be done for if they looked that nice back then. Chuck had his sword buckled backwards.

"We'll have to roll around in the dirt before going through." Sam thought aloud.

"Good call….Sergeant." Chuck teased.

"You too Captain. Or Captain Kangaroo is more like it." Sam teased back. "*This is going to be cool.*" Sam thought anxiously.

They made their way to the gate and rolled around as promised. Their packs and equipment were rubbed down with dirt as well. They both cautiously peered through the gate. The shimmering gave way to a view of a massive column of American troops marching down a dusty, old road.

They cautiously stepped through to find an American private standing on the other side. Worn and sullen in appearance, he appeared to have no blood in his cheeks at all. The smell of sulfur was heavy in the air. Only the slight aura above his head and the jolt of joy in Sam's being gave the Angel away. The Angel feigned a smile and his aura dimmed again.

"This is not a happy time for that Angel." Chuck whispered.

"This way gentlemen." The Private spoke. "Just catch up to the end of the column and blend in. We're marching now." The Angel pointed to the column, shook his head and blended into the formation. They glanced at each other in disbelief. Neither one knew what to expect, but both knew it wasn't what they thought it would be.

Slowly, they fell in at the end of the column. Ragged men, with little hope in their eyes, were all around. Flashes and thunder loomed ahead. The beginning of the column crested the hill. Then a few men in front of them marched over…

Then, all Hell broke loose. Multiple cannon shot tore through the men in front of them as though they were mere weeds. Men dove everywhere and screaming calls for advancement were made. Cries and yells filled the void that the pressure from the thunder left.

Two officers in front screamed something loudly, but the sounds of the volleys were too much for them to understand. They saw men forming lines in front and marching in unison forward. A third, mounted officer with his sword out led from the left. "Advance!!!!" A cannon roared and the horse and officer were gone.

It was absolutely horrifying. Worse than anything Sam had seen in his three tours in the Middle East. He began to realize that this was probably a very bad idea. "Remember our deal!" Chuck yelled over the cannon fire. "Remember, we get to see, but NOT fire!"

"OK!" he screamed back. Both men were less than two feet apart but the roar of the weapons and the repeated waves of pressure from the cannon tore through their ears. The smell of sulfur was saturating. "This is more combat than I've ever seen in all of my real life!" Sam yelled out. "Look at the size of this battle! I say we get the Hell out of here!"

"Good call! But take a look around. At least see what you came to see!" Chuck yelled back.

"All I want to see is home!" Sam yelled back quickly.

"Then just wish for it!" Chuck screamed back over the volleys.

Sam did as ordered. "Look! The gate's next to the farm house over there. Chuck screamed. Let's make a run for it! They started to sprint, but Chuck stopped them after a few steps. "Wait! Wait! Make the box like I did in the hospital room!" Chuck panted out.

"What??? Are you crazy????" Sam cried incredulously.

"Just do it! Quickly!" Once again, Sam nervously did as told. He drew the box but nothing appeared.

"Now stand next to me. Hurry!!!" Chuck yelled out.

Sam did as told. "Look this way and smile!" Chuck commanded. Sam looked at where he drew the box. There was a light blue outline, but nothing inside.

But Sam did not smile. He quite simply didn't understand what the Hell was going on. The old man must've lost his mind. The only look on Sam's face was a look of petrified uncertainty. This was highlighted by a quick flash of exploding bright light.

"What are you friggin' doing? That was close!" Sam yelled. "Let's get the F outta here!"

Both men ran like never before. Their fear turned into elation; joy that only men who have survived combat can know. It was the absolute feeling of being alive. They laughed hysterically as the adrenaline pumped through their veins.

Just feet away from diving into the gate, Sam felt a hot searing pain in his left leg. The pain shot like a red hot poker had been run through him. He immediately fell just short of entering. Chuck threw down his rifle and quickly scooped him up. As they dove through, another stray shot entered the gate with them.

They fell through and landed very, very, hard on the soft grass. Both men stayed down, their hands over their heads. It took a second to collect their thoughts and then looked at each other in disbelief.

Sam's left leg was thoroughly soaked with blood. The blue uniform pant leg betrayed a rather sizable bullet hole. Chuck started laughing at him, which Sam could not understand. "What are you doing dammit? I've been shot!"

"Have you now?" Chuck continued laughing. "Better check." Sam sat up and felt down his leg. There was no wound. There was a hole and blood on his pant leg, but there was no pain.

Sam laid back down and let out a long whistled breath. "Holy sh…."

Both men looked at each other and laughed that old deep, familiar family laugh. "Man, I wish my brother had been here for that one!" Sam laughed aloud.

"Yeah." Chuck replied. "Leave it to an old Marine to make his first Heavenly adventure a war zone. I knew I joined the Navy for a reason!"

Both men took a minute and began to sit up. They collected their gear which was absolutely strewn all over the grass. "Look, you were shot over there." Chuck pointed back toward the gate. "But when we went through the gate, you entered back into our reality. So, your body is as before you left. But look at that tree in front of us." Sam saw a branch had been snapped off. Directly behind the tree, a small, shiny ball was lodged in the wall of his house.

"This is just crazy." Sam let out as he laid there. Both men didn't move for a long while and enjoyed the warmth of the afternoon sun on the grass. "Wanna stay over for dinner Grand….Ummm Chuck? Something tells me there's steaks on the Barbie."

"Calling me Grandpa is fine. Or Chuck; It's your call. And yes, I'll use the guest bedroom and take an extremely long, hot shower. But before I do, I think a VO and water will be most useful. By the way, you may want to check your den. I think you'll find something new on the wall."

Sam gave Chuck wary look and slowly the two men made it to the house. Chuck went to the guest bedroom and Sam went to his office. Up on the wall, he saw the pictures from his old life. All great memories that came rushing back to him. These memories were all encased in polished grey metal frames on the wall.

On the wall to his left was a single picture in a solid gold frame. There were two men in it; One man toothily smiling into the camera, wearing the bars of a Captain on a dirty, blue uniform. Next to him, was a very confused and scared Sergeant, his eyes and mouth both wide open. He was clearly looking at something of interest off to the side.

Sam chuckled softly to himself. He would never live this down. What a day. He decided that… Chuck…. was right. A drink was a good idea. He had to find the bar. Every member of his family had a home bar, so he knew it had to be somewhere—hopefully.

He found it next to the kitchen and was going to make himself the usual Captain and Coke. But instead, he found a covered basket on the marble bar. "*Oh yeah.*" He remembered. He thought of a bottle of Captain Morgan's rum, opened the basket and there it was. "*How very, very cool.*" Sam thought.

"Thank God!"He said aloud.

He stopped in his tracks and looked up. He half expected to hear something in return or get hit with a lightning bolt. He just chuckled as he walked into the bedroom. This was going to take some getting used to.

Downing the stiff drink, he made his way to the upstairs bedroom. A beautiful four posted bed with satin sheets took center stage. To the left, a fireplace with timber ready to be lit was topped with an Oaken mantel complete with more pictures from his youth.

He opened a side door to find a marble bathroom complete with stunningly white terry towels. "Thank God they're not initialed" he joked aloud. He never was one for being….overly….ostentatious.

The steaming shower was just the ticket needed for this most of unusual days. After a long shower, he found the bathrobe that matched the towels. He knew that it wouldn't be long until the alcohol kicked in fully and he'd be done for the night. As he slipped into bed a slight knock roused him.

"Sam, looks like your done. Let's do dinner tomorrow--I'm headin' out" Chuck said as he peeked in. "Goodnight buddy, see ya for breakfast tomorrow?"

"Sounds great Grandpa." He replied dazedly. He looked over to find a hand turned Mickey Mouse table top clock like he had as a child.

"0900 Grandpa?" Sam said while drifting off.

"9 A.M. it is" Chuck smiled in reply. Chuck turned down the wall mounted gas lamp on his way out and Sam started to slip away. The open windows provided a gentle breeze that carried the scent of jasmine. *"Unbelievable."* He allowed himself to settle. Then, the typical Sam came through. *'Maintenance around here is going to be a bitch"* he thought as he quickly drifted off.

"What do you think Mother?" The young, brown bearded man asked almost angrily. He sat in a large golden throne. Long ribbons of purple and silver flowed behind him. To his left, a plain but beautiful woman in a shimmering blue robe watched contently. Her dress portrayed the moving galaxies in its deep blue and golden hues.

The young, bearded man looked down at him with a slight scowl and then eventually with a slight grin. Everything seemed to be happening in slow motion. "I think there's much to be saved here." she said. "And he did have the medallion on him."

"But there's also been almost as much hurt as help." The man replied. He looked at Sam with the disappointed and worried face that all fathers have at many times in their lives. "Heaven he is not, but I don't think HE shall not have him either." He glanced at her and she nodded he head.

"What's happening here? Oh my God.... "

Sam awoke abruptly and sat straight up. Outside, was the beautiful sound of birds chirping on his window sill. He looked around and realized that he had been dreaming. "Roses, I smell roses." Where is that coming from? He said aloud to himself.

He swung his feet down to the cold wooden floor. He could hear a slight chiming outside. Still stunned, he slowly walked down to investigate the sound. Rubbing his eyes in the warm morning sun, he noticed a small tin mailbox next to the gate. He opened it and couldn't believe his eyes.

"A newspaper? Sweet!" Sam almost tripped running back inside. He lit the gas stove and found the appropriate kettle and coffee inside the shelves. Starting eggs and *real* bacon, he decided that this was going to be a very good day. He opened the newspaper to inspect this "Midtown Journal." Oddly enough, the front page consisted of largely good news.

The material for the paper seemed almost to be made of parchment. The words and paragraphs were all aligned and when Sam looked closely he could see the outlines of black where the words had actually been pressed onto the paper. "*You gotta be kidding me, a no-kidding printing press????*" He thought with incredulity.

The more he thought more about it, it all did kind of make sense. No electric and only natural gas powered this and that. Even gunpowder didn't work here. "These new Midtown rules." Sam contemplated aloud. "I gotta get used to this new way of life."

The front page spoke of multiple good deeds and interesting stories of some of the new people arriving daily. Ironically, Sam didn't make the news. "*Ha! Underestimated even here.*" He joked to himself.

On the bottom of page one, there was an article of a brick layer who was smashed as he was working on a building. "*Well, he must have chosen to do this to work off his sins.*" Of course, the article ended happily as the man was vaporized and woke up in his bed. *"Those Midtown rules again…"* He thought.

Page two was a list of arrivals and a smaller list at the bottom of people who they think went "up". Eyewitness accounts of people who were thought to have known people they felt were getting closer. Lucky people who went to church one day and were seen being engulfed in the spiritual fire one last time.

While the flames were not entirely uncommon, it was uncommon for the person to disappear entirely. It was "known" then that the person had a one way ticket up. This went on for a few pages. Then there were some common articles before funny pages and the crossword. Finally, on the back page, was a list of folks that had been unaccounted for by anyone for quite some time. But this list had a darker inkling.

This was a list of people who were known recidivists of the darker ways of life. Crime, sin and defiance of God were acts of their pasts. Finally, one day, they just weren't around anymore. It is believed that these people found their way downstairs. These poor souls were never heard from again.

"*Man.*" He thought. "*I better keep it together.*" After scarfing down the bacon, eggs and coffee, he got ready for the day. "Wonder what Grand…I mean, Chuck's up to today." Sam thought. He looked up and made a huge clapping sound like the opening of the cave for Aladdin. "Ali Ali oxen free, Grandpa c'mon over!"

He felt a little ridiculous doing this, but evidently there were no real rules. He waited a second and nothing happened. This, of course, made him feel supremely stupid. He started to think of another way to conjure up ol' Chuck when he heard the bell ringing on the gate outside.

"Come in!" Sam yelled.

"I heard my bell ring and checked my mailbox. Looks like your getting the hang of this invite thing." Chuck said with a smile. He had on a red silk bathrobe, coffee and the paper. "What's the deal kiddo? Let's eat some of your eggs."

"Nothing really…." Sam half lied as they both sat down. "I was just reading the paper and saw how frequently people…… change status here. See, I don't necessarily want to go upstairs for a while. I'm not saying that I don't want to eventually, it's just that since I'm beginning to feel comfortable here, I'd like to be here if and when my family arrives….Ya know?"

"Ahh…." Chuck knowingly replied. "Well Sam, I think what your feeling is even more fear of the unknown. It's not unusual to fear….progress. But it's gonna happen one way or the other; change, that is."

Chuck took a sip of coffee and continued on. "But I can guarantee one thing. You will not progress "up" until you're ready to. And only you and *HE* will know when that's gonna happen. So don't worry, I hear that you'll gradually feel lighter and lighter.

Toward the end, you'll actually "feel" an… opaqueness of your being. This will happen just before your final transition. You will need your body and this world less and less each day—Ok?"

"Ok" Sam replied awestruck.

"So, what else is on your mind?" Chuck looked over the paper while sipping his coffee.

"Well, I'd like to see my family and look into any formalized jobs that I can do around here. Oh, don't get me wrong. The battle trip was incredibly cool, but I don't want to lose myself in dreams when I still think that I have a very real responsibility yet to achieve."

"What do you mean?" Chuck leaned closer.

"Well, one day my daughter will be here as well. I'm not sure, maybe she will go straight up, but I'm assuming very few actually do. Is that correct?" Chuck nodded inquisitively. "Ergo, I'm still a dad. And being a dad means setting the par. I'd like to at least be able to explain certain lessons to her like you did to me. That should mean working on myself and helping others. Or do I got the whole thing wrong?" Sam asked shrugging his shoulders.

"No. No. That's fine. Your eternity is yours to figure out. I, for the record, like the plan. So what were you thinking?" Chuck asked with an interested inflection.

"Well, how 'bout a guardian Angel job? Is that full time? Can I still do other stuff like the battle trip and chill here as well?" Sam was a little unsure of himself now.

"Sure you can. But You sure you wanna do this so soon? I mean, you just got here." Chuck said a little worriedly.

"Maybe you're right. I don't know. I just don't want to let anyone down. But I certainly don't want to start something I can't finish."

"It's really not that big of a deal." Chuck quickly replied. "You just look in on 'em when they need you. There's also usually more than one of them around. Basically, when you sign up for the job, you live your life up here. But when a....guardian Angel....situation arrives, you are instantly sent to their side.

That's really the extent of the job; you influence them by guiding them spiritually. And on the very rare physical exception, you may be able to make them, or the people around them, actually physically move something-- to increase their safety of course."

"No kiddin?" Sam asked.

"No kidding." Chuck replied flatly.

"Remember when you were eight and you were crossing the road to go to elementary school? You were tired and oblivious to the world around you. As you walked during the "Walk" sign, a green LTD ran the light because he was late for work. When you looked up half way through the road, you noticed a side mirror pass not one inch in front of your chest. As the car sped by, the actual finger pull thingy on your heavy jacket bounced off the mirror."

"I remember." Sam said with a sigh. "The whole thing happened in slow motion. Like well, when I ah...well....died."

"Yeah." Chuck sensed his hurt. "But it wasn't yet your *time.* So your Angel was called in a few seconds before the collision. She was able to slow you down while the driver's Angel was able to make the driver move the steering wheel an inch to the right. Otherwise, you'd be road kill."

"Nice." Sam replied. "You still have a certain way with words." They both laughed that deep family laugh. "O.K., Let's spend some time together, just tooling around. But that does sound like something I'd like to do. Where's the local recruiting office?" Sam offered with a smile.

After some time in Midtown, they finally both agreed it was time to meet at St. Patrick's and get at it. In the morning, they would speak to a priest who would show Sam the ropes.

Chapter Nine

May They Get.... "Fried"

Breakfast in the Irish quarter did not disappoint. Eggs and sausage accompanied by a deep stout beer made for a fine breakfast. The two men made small talk after reviewing the newspapers. They'd go to the cathedral in Midtown and see if a priest could find time to see them. The drive over was just as amazing as the rest of Midtown itself. It seemed everyone here loved their cars. But oddly enough, no actual gas stations dotted the cityscape itself.

"No gas stations?" Sam asked?

"Don't worry." Chuck replied "For some odd reason, the cars never go empty and the tires never wear down. You'll find the same for your yard and home. Of course, if you need to do those things, just go to the large basket in your garage. You'll find all the support you need."

"Of course." Sam smiled. "Wish I woulda had a few of those baskets in South Carolina."

"Me too!" Chuck exhaled. "But I probably would've had a real bad drinking problem." Chuck winked in reply.

Upon arriving at the cathedral, Sam couldn't help but be in awe over the sheer size of it. Golden apses reached to the sky, blending into the beautiful purple roofing. The architecture blended Greek, Moorish, Italian and a variable of other influences. The absolute beauty of it all stunned him.

As they were standing, the bells rang out their deep tonal ring eleven times. "Good, we're early." Chuck stated. "Daily mass here is also at twelve. We probably have time to speak to the padre." As they were walking up, Sam noticed something totally unexpected, it was an actual beggar.

The man reeked of liquor and wore tattered clothes. Sam looked over at Chuck with a look of incredulity. "The poor will always be with us." Chuck said reading his intentions. Sam walked over to the man and reached in his pocket for money, but of course, there was none.

Concerned, Sam half angrily turned to his grandfather and whispered. "Please walk with me Grandpa. How the Hell is this possible? Here? I know we're not in Heaven, but the meek shall inherit and all that?"

"Think it through Sam; you are here in Midtown—not Heaven. You have been given all those things that were important to you. Things that made you comfortable from your Earthly life because thats all you knew. Yet, spiritual advancement happens only when you learn to "wean" yourself from Earthly "things" and move up the spiritual ladder. So, why is he here?"

Sam pondered the man from afar and inferred: "He is here panhandling, because that's all he knew? This is what makes him happy?" Sam couldn't believe it.

"Correct." Chuck replied. "Who knows? Maybe he was actually very well to do on Earth, but suffered from mental problems. Maybe not. Maybe he has a nice home here. I don't know. I do know there's no mental illness here, so that is out. One thing's for certain, he enjoys the interaction." Chuck took a second and looked at Sam square in the eyes.

"Remember, a man's outcome is not necessarily equal to his income."

"*Damn, every now and again I forget how wise he is.*" Sam thought. "Well, can we offer him coffee or something?" Sam asked.

"Sure," Chuck replied. "I'd be less than happy if you did."

Sam, Chuck and the beggar spoke for a few minutes; the beggar declined the coffee as he had a covered basket next to him. They sat for a few minutes and instead the beggar produced coffee for them. The beggar spoke mildly to Sam as he stood up to leave. "One second sir-- You're new here, correct?"

"That obvious, huh?" Sam joked in reply. "I'm trying to become one of those guardian Angels."

"Have a seat." The beggar offered. When he did, the man put his hand on Sam's shoulder and began to explain how to make a vision box. They sat there for a while on the church steps. By the time Sam was done, Sam could now show images of whatever he was trying to explain "Amazing." Sam thought. He thanked the beggar profusely and started walking away with Chuck.

"And all because I took time to have breakfast with a beggar." Sam noted aloud to no one.

"Well, he does work in mysterious ways." Chuck joked and pointed up.

Practicing his new ability while walking, Sam and Chuck absent-mindedly walked through the massive front doors of the church. Without warning, a slight warmth started tingling in Sam's feet and extending quickly through his entire body. He looked down to see a mix of bright yellow, red and orange flames quickly engulf his entire body. It happened too quickly for him to scream and it didn't matter anyway—there was very little pain. As fast as the searing flames encased him, they also went out.

Still, it did hurt Sam some and it took a huge toll on his….body. Sam fell over and sat next to the stairs leading to the choir loft. He looked over at Chuck who was just as surprised as he was.

"Must've been the beggar." Chuck mumbled with a mixed smile that showed some concern. A brown robed priest ran up and was visibly taken back at the two walking in. He quickly moved to Sam's side. "Sit my son, sit. You ok? Hold on. I'll get water."

"Yes sir….Umm….Father." He was thoroughly confused. His skin was as clammy as he'd ever felt it. He could've swore that he actually saw through himself for a second.

"Did I just get "fried?"

The priest broke into a smile and simply nodded. "You alright? Need some of this water?"

The priest poured out some sparkling fresh water from a stone urn into a stone cup. It seemed to be the coolest and freshest water Sam had ever tasted.

"So." The priest continued, "Chuck, today's not Sunday and we have a half hour before mass, so what can I do for you two?"

"Well Padre." Chuck responded. "Yonder grandchild there wants to volunteer to be a guardian Angel. Got any openings?"

The priest smiled at Sam and nodded. "There's always room for more. The rules are pretty basic: You live your life here. You help out, out there. You come and go when you want, but you may "feel" a call if there's a need from the person. You then get "snapped" into their world when there's a threatening situation. This is, of course, unless it's God's time for them to go."

"Sounds good." Sam replied. His strength was now slowly regaining after the intense incident. "When do I start?"

"Now."

The last thing Sam felt was a hand on his shoulder from behind. An intense feeling of joy and love shivered through his body as he saw the priest and his grandfather quickly pull backward. He was shot through a swirling tunnel of white that lasted only a second. He looked down to see that he was standing on a grassy hill on a beautiful summer day.

Next to him stood a woman traditional full body Muslim dress. All her skin was covered except her hands and eyes. "You O.K.?" She chuckled.

"Umm. Yeah, just a little taken back, that's all. Wait! Aren't you a Muslim???" Sam felt immediately sorry for his outburst. Empty silence surrounded his downturned face.

"Don't worry Sam, you're not the first. Just remember that we all serve God in our own way. My way was to volunteer to be a guardian for the Christian guardian Angels. In this way, I can spread tolerance in both worlds. Something that maybe needed…yes?"

Sam half ashamedly looked down and nodded his head. There was still so much to learn.

"I'm sorry if I offended…"

She raised a hand to cut him off. In a cheerful voice she gave him a reprimand "If we were all perfect, we would not be here. Would we?" Her brown eyes betrayed her humor and Sam felt better about it.

"Now then Christian, Let us see what the Angels have in store for you. Ahh... there... that's the one." In the distance, Sam could see a small boy of no more than nine or ten years old. He was sitting all alone on a swing set, his bike lying next to him. He was looking down and rocking ever so slowly back and forth.

"What's wrong with him?" Sam asked worriedly.

"Nothing really—life I guess. He's the smallest of his class. Not the best or the brightest, but has a good heart. However, dark thoughts fill his head.

He has been bullied his entire life and his parents are divorcing. It's not a good time for him. You have to...help... to keep him going."

"Me? How?" Sam asked, shrugging his shoulders.

"That is up to you. That is your part of the journey. Oh, and when you want to leave, just think of home. A' Salaam."

Behind her a beautiful stone gate appeared. Sand spilled through the opening and he could see tall fig trees and a tent in the distance. As she stepped through the shimmering vision, it all disappeared. He just stood there dumbfounded.

"What the Hell have I gotten myself into." He mumbled to himself. He took a second and turned around in a quick military style and marched off toward the boy. Sam confidently thought, *"I can do this. Let's get you squared away."*

As he approached the boy he quickly rethought that approach. *"I can't do this."* He thought. *"I have no idea what to do."*

He looked at the boy and felt pangs of sorrow and fear. Studying the boy up and down, he sat on the swing next to him. A gentle breeze pushed Sam slightly back and forth.

A revelation quietly inspired him. "O.K., I get it. Just like before. I just have to get to know this kid and help the hurt, then maybe he'll get better. I just have to will myself and something completely unexpected will happen to or for him right?" he realized he was looking up and talking to no one. The child just looked down with a somber view. It was so quiet.

"Look buddy, hang in there. Divorce and bullies suck. Why don't we get out of this lonely place and go home to your folks. Your Mom or Dad or whatever…Man, this sucks. But being alone for too long is no good either kid. C'mon kid, get on the bike."

The boy just continued looking down and kicking a stone with his feet. Sam felt absolutely powerless. "Why isn't this working buddy?" He stood up angrily. "How can I help?" As he said "help" he put his hand on the boy's shoulder. The child looked up at the sun under his large baseball cap and sniffled back a tear. Sam could swear he was looking right at him.

The boy immediately got up and got on his bike and started pedaling as Sam had suggested.

"No way…" He mumbled.

As the boy started pedaling faster, Sam starting running after him. To his surprise, he was keeping up and not even breathing hard. He looked down to see that his feet weren't even touching the ground.

"No way!" he said again. This time, with an incredible yell.

He grabbed hold of the back of the child's bike. To his surprise, he started to glide and became completely horizontal as the boy gained full speed. The boy's orange flag on the back of his bike slapping wildly about as Sam dodged it while holding on.

Sam's "body" also flapped around like the flag as the wind increased. He let out a childish scream of excitement. When he did, the boy also let loose a huge whistle and smiled as he jumped the curb off the road. Sam held on for dear life.

In the distance another man viewed the spectacle and shook his head with a smile. A large man, he wore a stripped bowling shirt and jeans. This would be of no unordinary consequence except for the fact that he was perched on top of a flag pole fifty feet up while watching.

As the boy slowed down, Sam became vertical again and slowly floated to the ground. Trying in vain to coordinate his feet, he tumbled head over heels. But there was no pain as he actually tumbled above the ground without touching. He laid there for a second and looked up.

Standing above him was a man in his twenties. He had a large football player type build and he held his huge arm out.

"Need a hand?" The stranger asked with a smile.

"Thanks" Sam replied. "I'm guessing that if you can see me you're a guardian Angel too."

"That's correct." The man replied. "New to this, are we?"

"Yes I am." Sam sheepishly replied. "Love the weightless thing."

"Yeah, It is kinda cool. But there's lots more to discover too. Just make sure that you remember why you're here, ok?" The man's reminder hit him hard.

"Oh my God. I don't even know where he is! Your right! I don't even know his name!"

The man held up his hand. "Don't worry. Just think about him. Think about where he is right now." Sam did as ordered and saw the stranger pull backwards. The large man began to get smaller as the world swirled around him.

"By the way!" The man yelled out. "Your Aunt says Hi! We'll see ya' son!"

Sam tried to fight the pull in the swirl, but it was too late. He was standing on a coffee table in the middle of someone's living room. He said aloud "I'll be damned. Wait. Bad choice; I'll be durned. Uncle Paul-- He looked good!" His broad smile continued as he stepped down. When he started to walk through the rest of the house, a set of pictures on the fireplace mantle caught his attention.

The pictures were all of the boy and his mother. Obviously and painfully absent were any pictures of his father. Slight, strained smiles covered the two faces. But no real joy was there.

Sam looked at the pictures for a long time. Thoughts of his own divorce and those of divorces around him made him reflect on his own life.

"*Damn.*" He thought sadly. "*I've got my work cut out for me.*"

He found the boy in the kitchen eating a peanut butter and jelly sandwich. His mother doted on him while doing dishes at the sink. "Your father called. He's not going to be able to make it again. He says the trip is going to be longer than expected. Sorry Mikey—look, we'll go to the ballgame together instead ok?"

Mikey just sat there with his head hung low and ate slowly. He finished half the sandwich and dropped the rest in the trash. "It's Ok Mom. I'm gonna look for my friends? OK? I'll see ya in a few hours."

She bravely put on a smile and held the boy's face close. "He does love you Mikey. He does." Mikey nodded and grabbed his ball glove from the table. As he shuffled out the front door, he slowly mounted the bike and began riding down the street. Sam stood there in utter despair. "Damned fool father." Sam muttered aloud.

The boy's mother stood there, head hung low and began quietly sobbing. She slowly rubbed the same clean plate again and again. Slowly, a shimmering light appeared next to Mikey's mother. Out of nowhere, a woman dressed in a simple house coat appeared next to her. She stood next to the woman and looked at her, giving Sam just a slight glance out of the corner of her eye.

"You are loved Sally." The woman spoke softly. "You and Mikey will be alright—I promise." The boy's mother wiped her eyes and stared out of the kitchen window. The guardian Angel next to her just stared out as well. Sam suddenly felt very obtrusive and slowly walked out of the room, tears streaming from his eyes.

He had felt her pain as real as he felt the boys. He now understood what it must've been like when he hurt others in his life. The pain that he had felt magnified by the solemn promise he had given before God. He also now understood that he was here not only for the boy's benefit, but to learn some painful lessons himself. Sam took a second to collect himself and took a deep breath.

He glanced back into the kitchen to see the boy's mother sitting down drinking a cup of coffee. The guardian Angel only smiled at Sam. Sam smiled back and tried to think of the boy.

"*Where is he?*" He couldn't get out of there fast enough. Thankfully, the kitchen scene swirled away and Sam found himself standing next to a swing set by a baseball diamond.

"You take him, I'd rather have a girl!" A large boy pointed and laughed at Mikey. They all laughed and Mikey looked down.

"Fine. Mikey your with us—forget that jerk." Another boy replied in anger. Mikey grabbed his glove and walked over. The boy next to him took a step away from him and whispered to no one. "*Weirdo.*"

The game started and as expected Mikey was relegated to right field. '*Hopefully, no one will hit the ball out here.*" Mikey thought to himself. Oddly enough, it was the same thought that absolutely everyone had about the situation.

It wasn't just that the boy was athletically challenged. It was more of the equation of development. He was simply behind the power curve of the other boys and also had not yet developed his hand to eye coordination. That coordination is only achieved through practice. And you either need older friends or a father for that. This, of course, led to the boy's horrible self-esteem. It could be a vicious circle.

Luckily for all, a few innings went by and no one actually did hit the ball to Mikey. When it became his turn at bat, he took the oversized helmet and heavy bat and took a few practice swings. The force of the bat and lopsided helmet almost made the boy fall as he struggled to steady himself. Mikey heard the chuckles from the other boys but approached the plate bravely anyway.

"*I'm not going to hit the ball.*" Mikey thought.

"He's not going to hit the ball." The catcher mumbled.

"*Hell, he can barely level the bat.*" Sam thought as well.

The boy stood there at home plate determined to prove them wrong.

He knew that he was not going to quit. He knew that one day he'd hit the damned thing. That one day his dad would come home for good and be proud of him. That one day he would forgive him for not being the best son in the world and just come home. That one day…

"Strike Three!" the older boy yelled behind the pitcher.

The boy hadn't even swung.

Chapter Ten

R.I.P.? Hell, I Can't Even Get Through.

After the usual ball game, various plans were made by the boys to do this or that. None of who invited Mikey to attend. Only Matt, the nicest of the boys made a genuine effort. "Wanna come over Mikey? Mom's got pizza."

The other boys looked disapprovingly at Mikey and he could feel his embarrassment level rising. "Uhhh, thanks but I gotta go. My dad's waiting for me."

As he rode away, Sam shook his head and just followed him. "This is how it all starts Mikey-- just one more lie. We have got to get you past this." He followed the boy home and made sure he made it in safely. Mikey went through his usual routine of microwave pizza bites and soda. His mother was already passed out on sleeping pills. When he went to take a shower, Sam knew his watch for the day was probably complete.

Soberly, Sam muttered, "*Home please.*"

Outside the back window he could see his gate. He sadly went through the shimmering portal and walked into his yard. The dogs ran up to him and started bothering him. Sam just patted them and walked directly to his room. He just wanted to sleep.

"*This Midtown stuff isn't exactly Heaven after all.*" Exhausted, he was quickly asleep.

This interaction between himself and Mikey went on for months. Sam just couldn't seem to do anything to influence Mikey's world like he had done with his wife or daughter. He had been allowed to look in on them from time to time and even help them on some occasions. But there was nothing he could do for this boy.

He tried to console himself in the fact that his daughter was progressing nicely and was now in her first year of college. Hell, she even went to the occasional church service. While his wife also now carried on day to day activities and seemed to be on the other side of the initial depression.

"Why was I able to influence them, but not Mikey?" Sam asked Chuck as they ate their usual weekly breakfast.

Chuck took a second and peered over his coffee cup, "I'm not exactly sure. I've asked around, but I think it's because you have no personal connection with him" Chuck responded. "All this time you have tried what, exactly?"

"Everything." Sam replied. "Yelling, praying, suggesting crying, begging—you name it. I just don't know what else to do."

"OK. Chuck replied. "I think I may know what's happening: You see, with your family, you've always had… a spiritual connection. You just don't automatically have that with this boy. I think in order to influence him, you have to be part of his "soul". Make that happen and maybe you can help."

"Well thanks a lot. I have no idea how to go forward on that one. How do I establish a connection with a boy who cannot see or hear me?"

"Hey, I never said it was going to be easy." Chuck replied softly. "You been goin' to church and askin' the big man?"

"Every Sunday." Sam replied. "No more flames of enlightenment either. And I'm definitely not ready for any further adventures in time or space either. Grandpa, this boy is sliding into a real depression. I've got to do something before it gets too late."

Chuck drained his coffee and started to get up. "Perhaps you have to change something in yourself before you can help him. If the boy hasn't changed and the world around him hasn't changed, then the only thing left that can change is you, right? Think about it. Perhaps you are the one who's not "ready" to connect, instead of the other way around."

Sam watched him leave and tossed down his napkin in frustration. "*Well that's just friggin' great. Sometimes that old man is full of Wisdom and sometimes crap. But this sounds like wisdom to me.*" And it was frustrating.

Mulling over the earlier conversation for days, Sam finally went to go see Mikey. As usual, he was alone and riding his bike. Sam really felt for this kid. There must be something he could do. In the past, Sam had done everything he could think of for the boy: Suggestions, prayer, yelling, the works. Finally, he started to get desperate.

Seeing another obviously lonely boy playing not thirty feet away by himself hit Sam like a ton of bricks. Didn't Mikey see that this kid was hurting too? With frustrated tears in his eyes, he tried to grab the boy by both shoulders and hug him. "Look Mikey, you have been so surrounded by your own selfish problems that you never really looked to see that other people around you can be just as lonely!"

As the words tumbled from Sam's mouth, he heard for the first time what he knew to be a real truth. A real truth that applied to Sam as well. He was giving advice that he had very rarely taken himself. "Dammit Grandpa. Not even here, and still teaching…"

Mikey put down his father's beloved baseball glove and walked straight to the other boy. "Hey, I'm Mikey, wanna play catch or somethin?"

Sam was astonished at this radical change of events. From the corner of his eye, he saw *her* appear-- That beautiful lady in cosmic blue again. The same Woman cloaked in what appeared to a dress made of the actual stars themselves. She looked at him and smiled radiantly. Her radiance of love and happiness consumed him.

"Finally. Now think." She commanded softly. Instantly he was transported into a vision of his whole life in Midtown and that of his life before on Earth. He saw the whole world transpire around him and saw the emotional walls that he had built to keep everyone out. Then, he made the connection of Mikey's life and his own.

For the first time, Sam had actually both "physically and spiritually touched" another soul. He had genuinely cared for another human being that was not his family or a romantic interest. For the first time, he had let actual emotional, spiritual and physical contact happen. With the simple act of a hug, he had let down his walls, allowing both the boy and Sam to see beyond their problems. With this selfless act, Sam grew spiritually himself.

He looked at her after the vision and smiled. "I'm gonna get some of that fire stuff in church, aren't I?

She just smiled back and laughed. "Perhaps. Take nothing for granted. But I'm told that one gets used to it. There may be hope for you yet silver carrier." She disappeared as quickly as she appeared. "Silver carrier? What?" Sam tried to ask. As she evaporated, Sam noticed the familiar smell of fresh roses in the air.

He watched the boys play for a while and thought of home. "*This is going to be one Hell of a story for ol' Chuck.*" Later that night, Chuck and Sam discussed the story. Sam felt a sense of elation and joy in helping the boy. But Chuck was genuinely happy for both of them.

As usual, they both somehow managed to turn the experience into a few jokes and they laughed that same familiar family laugh. Chuck was especially fond of the fact that Sam suspected he might get "fried up" upon entering church.

"That's not exactly how it works!" Chuck teased. "When you think it's gonna happen, it doesn't and vice versa. But to see you worry about it like this is priceless."

"I know. I know." Sam replied happily. "But listen, I've now seen Angels, guardian Angels and even dead relatives. But who is the one lady who arrives every now and again?"

Chuck eyed him up for a moment and his eyes widened. "Blue dress? Shimmering stars with the actual galaxies floating in them?"

Sam eyed him with suspicion right back. "Now that you say it that way, yes…."

"She's one of the few actual physical beings up here. She has many names and titles, but to you—Mary. You know, mother of Jesus?

Sam sat back and started to blurt "What? Thee Mary? Why? How? Wow."

"Yep." Chuck replied flatly. "It's rare, but she can be everywhere at once. When the situation proves itself worthy, she will actually make an appearance. It seems she may have a slight interest in you—God only knows why." He joked openly.

"Me? But WHY? I wasn't even a good Catholic. What did I do???"

"Beats me." Chuck answered. "But something has drawn her to you. Better not screw it up." "Look, was she ever a patron saint to you? Think. Does she KNOW you for a specific reason?" As he was talking Chuck started to draw the vision box that he had used when they first met. But this time, only the blue powder-like outline existed. There was no scene inside. As Sam started to look deep within the box, a vision appeared.

It was a very somber scene at the hospital. His wife was given a manila folder to sign for by the morgue. In it, were all Sam' personal effects. She opened it, but just couldn't go through them. As she drove home crying, she swerved to avoid hitting another car. The envelope fell open and out spilled his wedding ring and wallet.

The wallet folded open to show a small glimmering object protruding from the center. It was the small silver medallion depicting the Virgin Mary. It was something he'd always believed in, but forgot about; the ultimate promise of forgiveness and deliverance. The scene showed the obvious connection and then disappeared.

"Oh my God, I'd completely forgotten." Sam declared.

"Well, that may very well be why you're here now and not somewhere more......heated." Chuck laughed. "But now you have a problem Sam. She kept her end of the deal. Will you keep yours?"

"Man--just a little more pressure please." Sam sighed.

"Look, just live your life. When she wants to be seen, she'll be seen. By the way, notice any other..... sense of familiarity? Perhaps a fragrance?"

"What?" Sam didn't understand.

"A flower, perhaps?" Chuck winked.

Sam quickly made the association in his head. "That's where the roses come from-- gotcha."

"Now back to your story; when will you see the boy again?" Chuck laughed.

The men talked for hours into the night. Sam had a few days until Sunday, but didn't want to wait. He wanted to go to church tomorrow to "get it over with." He rose early and went, but upon entering the church, nothing happened. He sat down at the mass confused and stayed after to speak to the priest.

The old grey bearded priest surprised Sam. "*Well, I suppose it makes sense humility wise…*"Sam thought to himself.

"What's going on son?" Sam told him the whole story with a depressed sigh. "I think I know what may be going on Sam. I suspect that you came here for naively selfish reasons. Your grandfather was right; only through humility does this happen. You do know that he has a very close "relationship" to the blessed Mother, right? He has been in here praying to her for all of you for years."

He patted Sam on the shoulder and walked to another needy soul. Sam, understanding his mistake, started out the door. If he hurried, he could still meet his Grandfather at his usual afternoon lunch at Ari's. "The old man is a clever bastard." Sam happily thought to himself.

He reached the door to the church and was stopped cold. The blinding blue bolt of shock went straight through him and the tingling started at the bottom to engulf him whole. Years of sin burned lightly in the flames and he held his arms out in a victory sign."

The feeling of absolute joy and love was undeniable. He fell down saturated with sweat and sat on the stairs leading to the choir loft just as he had done so many times passing out in church as a child. He was handed a cool cup of water from a stone chalice. The shimmering man with the sword and pale face smiled, winked and walked away.

He collected his thoughts and just sat for a while. It seemed like the more he learned, the less he knew. When enough strength resumed, he made his way home again. The afternoon naps that he loved on Earth would be very welcomed now. He was exhausted… but also……."lighter."

There was so much to ponder: How to improve his life, how to help the boy, when to go on another "jaunt", how to continue helping his family. As he sat on his back porch with his dogs, he looked over the large lake in the back yard. "*The only thing better would be a thunderstorm*" he thought. "*I Miss those growing up on the Great Lakes….*"

Slowly, the dark clouds began to form. Smoldering giants began bellowing above. He absolutely loved the energy of a storm above water.

He walked out onto the pier to be alone with nature, as the dogs definitely wanted no part in this insanity. He sat on the bench at the end of the pier and his mind began to wander.

But it began to wander in selfishness.

"*I wonder how my daughter's doing*? He wondered solemnly. He wished to be taken to her and ran to the gate to visit her, but was not allowed. The gate showed nothing.

"*After all I've been through! 'Damn! Why did the Angels only allow this to happen when they thought it was best? Who were they to deny him his daughter. Damn it! And after all I've been through. What about me! Aren't I better now! Who are they to deny me!*"

The more he thought about her, the more depressed and angry he became. As he walked back to the pier; the storm, sensing his feelings, began to churn violently. Lightening crashed on the water and the waves slammed against the pier. Sam sat there entranced in his own dark, selfish thoughts. Deeper and deeper his mind descended. "*Damn it*" He thought. "*All this love and cleansing and power and I'm still powerless to help those who I love the most.*"

"DAMN IT!!!" Sam screamed out.

His scream was amplified in the wind. It echoed back to him twice as large. He was feeding off of the storm and the storm, off of him. The amplified echo came back with an evil growl that was NOT of his making. Above him, he could see two eyes forming in the clouds. They looked directly at him they rolled violently like the clouds that built them. For the first time since arriving in Midtown Sam felt fear—real fear. Something evil was present.

He stood up and started to slowly walk backwards carefully. "*What the Hell is going on here? I didn't ask for all of this.*" The rain started heavily know, wind and hail and rain pelted him sideways, the wind was almost unbearable. Lightning and thunder cracked now once per second and were forming walls of blinding light all around him.

Directly above him were the eyes; Hollow, unmerciful, eyes, that watched him with intense hatred. They started to squint with the laughter that bellowed in the wind.

"Stop!!! Help!!!!" He screamed. But the raging winds drowned him out. The pelting rain felt like fingers digging into his skin. The bluish-green water crashed violently onto the pier. Sam tried to run back to land, but a wall of water enveloped him. Falling to the wood, be began to fight for breath. "Help." He spattered as he held onto the pier.

Above him flashed a blinding light. A literal tear formed in the sky directly above the clouds. Legions of radiant, winged warriors poured through the void. Flaming swords led those figures through dizzying paths through every part of the clouds. Through and through they danced, until every part of the clouds were gone.

They then flew into a massive formation resembling a large circle rotating directly above his head. As he laid there pitifully spitting up water, he could hear the most beautiful distant singing; Arias of alto and soprano that sang in practiced unison with each other. The portal, the literal tear in the sky, formed again. The inner circles entered, followed by the outer bands, until only one angel remained.

She floated down as the portal disappeared. A brilliant silver skinned woman with amber hair spoke to him in what he could only believe was a French accent "Sir, you have to be careful when making your environment here, OK? Oui? If you let in evil, evil will be let in. This, of course, was an accident. We will be here to protect you, but let's… temper our temper. Oui?"

She smiled and put her hand on his arm and pulled him to his feet. His fear left him and she winked. He felt absolute love again. "Besides, silver carrier, I think the boy needs your strength as does your daughter, oui?"

"Oui." Sam responded while looking down. There was still so much to learn.

"Look, she is fine and has graduation coming up soon. She will want you to see her then, OK? We can go then." She looked at him sympathetically.

"Oui." Sam said again humbly.

She started to walk away, but turned around halfway down the pier. "There is much to learn, but keep the faith. Believe in *him* like *He* believes in you." She sternly looked at him for one last time "And be very careful when making your environment. It will feed of your emotions. Rage, anger, pity, selfishness and loss can attract Lucifer and his minions. And we don't want that to happen again, Oui?"

"Oui." Sam answered with widened eyes. "*Again?*" Sam thought to himself. *'My God, that was Lucifer?* "

His saving Angel walked off the pier and left by the gate. She Stopped quickly to pat the dogs on the head. They seemed so obedient to her.

He started walking his soaked body back to land back when a terrible feeling overtook him. It was Mikey and he was in trouble. Thinking hard, he was instantly transported behind a row of snow covered bushes in someone's back yard. He saw the boy and a very pretty girl not fifty feet away. They were very close. It almost appeared as they were going to kiss. "Well, way to go!" He said quietly, "Why the Hell would this be a problem?"

Mikey moved in to kiss her, but she backed away. Obviously, she had differing ideas on the matter than he did. "What are you doing?" She yelled. "We're friends!"

"Oh my God, I'm so sorry!" But it was too late. A larger boy had also been watching from behind the bushes and was just looking for an excuse. He ran at Mikey and pounced on him. Mikey tried to defend himself, but the much larger boy just furiously punched him while sitting on his chest. Mikey held up his hands to cover his face. The humiliation of the beating was only reinforced by her watching it.

"Stop it!" she screamed. "He's my friend."

Sam started running at the scene, but was too far away to get there in time.

"You don't need friends like this!" The large boy yelled back. He held Mikey down and beat him furiously. Finally, he stopped his attack as the boy laid there defenseless. His face was a bloody mess.

"That's my friend, freak." He pretended to punch Mikey's face again. He knew that the boy would cower away from his raised fist. Instead, Mikey, looking through bloodied eyes, pushed the larger boy's hands aside and whispered out one last thing through broken lips.

"Screw you."

The large boy punched him one last time and proceeded to get up. Sam tried to stop it all, but was unable to do anything. The bully grabbed the girl by the arm and started pushing her towards the house. "Cmon!" He demanded. She started to go, but spun around mid stride. "I'm sorry Mikey. I really am." She truly was sorry for him. And Mikey knew it. It made everything that much worse.

He was just so damned tired of people feeling sorry for him. "*When will this stop?* He thought tiredly. "God? When will this stop?" He muttered aloud. He felt so very alone. "Why was I put so far away?" Sam screamed out.

He tried to pick Mikey up, but to no avail. The boy slowly got to his feet by himself. There was a party going on inside and Sam could see the other boy that had attacked Mikey. He was obviously bragging about the incident to his friends, the other boys laughing and shaking their heads.

Sam knew enough not to wish ill will on the larger boy, but couldn't help but feel sorry for the situation. "Don't worry Mikey." Sam spoke aloud "He will have to work this off. Trust me."

But it was of little solace as the battered boy peddled away on his bike. Sam spent the rest of the night and the next few days by Mikey's side. His mother, of course, wanted to know what the Hell happened to her boy. Mikey lied and told her it was football. This was about the tenth time that "football" had done this to him over the years.

Sam and Mikey continued with their spiritual stalemate for years. But Sam never left his watch. The situations where Mikey was in danger, either physically or emotionally had largely subsided, but Sam knew that all experiences would help to form the boy's sense of self. He also knew that the boy would soon be in his late teen years and would soon be graduating high school. There was even a girl who was genuinely interested in him, seeing as how Mikey was now finally growing into his "man's body."

Sam had also been allowed to see other scenes within his own family's life. His daughter had a beautiful graduation and he was there to see it all. She was doing so well now and had gone out of her way to visit him at the cemetery prior to the event. It was a cool spring day and the oak trees shaded her as she spoke: "Dad, I wish you were here." As she reflected on the green grass and cold headstone, a warming breeze blew a leaf into her hair.

"I am." Is all he could respond. "I am."

It was a sad time for them both, but he never left her without warmth in her heart-- she could always just "feel" him there. Also, he could see her resilience as she left each time. She truly was a blessing. How she was so strong at such an early age was a myth to him.

His wife, too, was doing better and better. She had begun to finally remember Sam instead of reliving Sam. That was always the key difference; remembering instead of reliving. She had started to attend a local church. Soon, she would be healed enough to move on.

He also had other wonderful times with his family and friends in Midtown; Times with his Grandparents, aunts, uncles and so on. But Mikey's evolution was his biggest concern. The boy now had a girlfriend and was having sex. Not only with her, but with other women as well. All while supposedly dating only one woman. Needless to say, "Mikey" had turned into "Mike" and was developing some of the same unhealthy habits Sam had as a young man.

His body had finally fully developed and with a vengeance. Mike was getting even on everyone. Boys were bullied and women were used. As he headed into his college years, his earlier experiences had turned him not only away from God, but almost entirely into a womanizing bully.

Mike was now in the habit of looking for a fight or a woman. And if he couldn't find one fix, then he'd definitely find the other. There could never be enough; never enough women to fight the anger, shame and feelings of being… less…. for all those years.

He also perfected the art of the "double life." He pretended to date only one girl, but kept "his options open". Which, of course, she had no idea about. Mike actually talked himself into the fact that he was protecting her.

Then one day, it happened. He had met "the one" and fell hard. She was a beautiful blonde with sparkling blue eyes. She was different from the other girls he had "dated". She was different……

He knew that if she was going to be the one that he was going to have to stop this "dating" around. So with no remorse, he quickly announced to "his girlfriend" that he had met someone else and left. Wound up in his own selfishness, it had never even occurred to him that he had destroyed not only her, but so many other women in his wake.

They "dated" and it went on for months. He thought everything was fine until he accidently opened her cell phone by mistake one day. There, he found openly sexual remarks showing in the inbox, which he unashamedly opened. It was even complete with a smiley face with puckered lips. It was from some guy named Jim who he'd never met before. Of course, it was her husband.

Then it occurred to him; he had been played; played like a fiddle. Everything that he had become, he hated.

Mike retreated to a shadowy depth in his mind that he'd never been to before. The absolute loneliness and realization that he was a total ass hit him hard. The worst part is that he had no recourse. No coping mechanism. Despite Sam's best intentions, he turned everyone and everything completely off. He was teetering on the edge of suicide.

The worst part was that Sam was constantly trying to get through but was absolutely powerless to do so. He knew that if it continued like this, Mike would run a similar path that had led to so much pain that he'd caused on Earth.

Sure, Sam had been able to prevent the occasional scrape and bruise in Mike's life, but not the real pain. He screamed at Mike, hugged him, swiped at him, prayed for him—but nothing worked. Mike just kept… slipping. He felt absolutely worthless to the young man now.

He knew that Mike would continue on this self destructive path and might actually do more harm than good in this life. And if his behavior became permanently coupled with his current lack of faith, well…. he could be in for the worse fate of all.

Shaking his head from side to side, Sam thought of his own life and how he'd been saved. How could he save "the man" that he had guarded as a boy. Sam just wanted to go home—to his new home. He had to get advice.

He had to think of something and soon. The gate appeared and he walked away beaten. He had to figure out a way to save this kid.

Chapter Eleven

Humility and Grace.

Back at his house in Midtown, Sam discussed the problem with Chuck. "I just can't seem to get through to him. I feel utterly useless."

"Sam, you've helped this young man since he was well… a boy. Right? He has been loved by his family and has had a few friends but has dealt with an inordinate amount of hurt. Correct?

"Yes." Sam was still confused.

"He has advanced to a point where you can no longer help him, because you have advanced to a certain….. point as well."

Sam was obviously confused. "But it's Mike who has the problems! Mike is doing these things! Mike isn't listening! What more can I….." He stopped himself cold. He felt like he was sitting on the end of the pier again.

"I can't fix him until I continue fixing me. Right?"

Chuck just sat there and looked at him. "Right." he replied flatly. Even he was surprised by the obvious hand of God at times.

Chuck continued, "Ya know, I think you were selected years ago for this job because of the similarity of traits and life's episodes. I *think* you are seeing yourself in the boy and being given a chance to help both him and you."

"And I thought this whole time it was just some wild coincidence." Sam replied astounded. "You'd think I'd know better by now, seeing as to where we live and all that."

"Look, I wasn't even sure myself until you provided the latest details. But now I think that if you want to make a connection to the ….um…young man…then you're gonna have to quit blaming others and forgive those people in your life that hurt you."

Tears began to well up in Sam's eyes. He quickly looked down. Chuck began to well up too. "Look, I don't know how to do it either. For me, I still have to forgive myself for ….things…done during the war that I cannot yet undo. But if you have it in you, I think you'll be able to influence Mike again."

Sam wiped his eyes with his sleeves and let out a slight laugh."Dead for years and still leaking." Both men chuckled and looked out into Sam's back yard. The lake was very placid in the Fall. "*Of course, it was always Fall here.*" Sam thought happily as he fought to dry his eyes.

After talking and thinking things through, Sam did one final check on his own family and Mike. He had spoken with Holy men from every religion he could find. They all had similar advice: Mutual forgiveness had to take place.

He had to come face to face with those who he had wronged and to those who had wronged him and who he had wronged. But seeing as how most of the people in his life were still alive, his only other option was to openly declare them forgived to God-- here.

He had to openly bear his soul, give and ask for forgiveness. From each one of those that he had hurt—one at a time. And as fate would have it, some of them were actually here. He would have to face one last challenge in order to help Mike, He would have to find ultimate humility himself.

As there was no standard way to do this, Sam thought that the Reverend's idea was the best: Find a small open church or chapel, invite those people who he had hurt and ask for forgiveness. So he did just that. Going through each catalog of his life using the vision box technique, he found each person who he had seriously wronged on Earth and invited them to a small mosque in the Islamic quarter. He figured that since he had participated in so many wars against countries of the Middle East, that this may be a fitting place to start.

Chuck wanted to go with Sam that fateful morning but knew he couldn't. He told Sam so, but also knew that he would sneak in later. They had their usual coffee and he took the long way in his Olds. He pulled up to the side of the mosque and asked for one small prayer of strength and walked in.

What Sam saw inside took him by surprise. Standing with their backs to the front door were about ten people who he had known in his life. But on the walls leading to the front of the church were literally dozens more. All of them sleeping or living their lives oblivious to the situation. They were all in their own individual vision boxes floating high on the walls.

As he took the scene in, an overwhelming sense of shame filled Sam's soul.

He slowly walked up through the center of the group. In the front, holy men representing what must have been a dozen denominations were up at the altar. They all walked slightly off as Sam walked up. Smiling sympathetically, they all stood behind him to give him strength. Sam continued to look down and fought hard with the urge to pass out and or run. He was just so ashamed to be there.

He glanced up to see just a few of the faces. Women scorned and men belittled; it had occurred to him that the hurt that he had received he had also paid forward in spades. *"Enough."* He thought. *"This has to stop."*

"I don't know what to do." He looked down and muttered.

"Well…." One of the men spoke up softly. "If *He* were here and *He* is….then I'd think that he'd start with outward forgiveness…. Gentlemen?" They all looked at each other and nodded with smiles.

"*This was not their first time doing this.*" Sam thought. His voice cracking, Sam started to speak with tears in his eyes.

"I…….uh……stand before each of you here today to………" silence filled the room and you could hear the breeze coming in from the open windows. He looked up to the expected angry faces, but there was an oddity before him; No one was angry. The faces that looked upon him were gently smiling. Even those souls on Earth that were sleeping were peaceful faces. He was filled with a small hope.

"I am so sorry. No. No. Words cannot explain…..Look, in order for me to ask your forgiveness I have to forgive myself and those who hurt me. So….here and now, I forgive them all. No more holding on to….."

Shivers shot through his spine. Absolute joy and love seared through his body. His feet began to tingle hotly. "I also ask you to forgive me…..the heat….. Please for…" His entire body was engulfed in purple, red and white flames. A loud singing surrounded all the patrons of the Mosque.

The beautiful singing became getting louder and louder. Sam felt the searing and waited for pain that really never came. It was more of a gentle heat. He thought that he holy men were holding him up during the process, but he was wrong, they were holding him down.

The holy men held him down and then reached out to the patrons. Everyone reached forward and gripped the shoulder of the person in front of them. A human chain formed and passed the flames outward.

Sam was just floating there—completely engulfed in fire.

The crescendo in the loft was that of a thousand voices giving praise above in an ancient language. The singing stopped suddenly and the whole room was eerily quiet. The flames extinguished themselves with a mighty wind that came from directly above. It blew Sam and the inner circle to the floor. Sam laid there stunned for a second and came to with the an Angel slapping him on the cheek.

"Better now?" The Angel said with a laugh. He slipped back through the crowd, who parted rows in honor of the man.

The holy men propped him up and offered him the coolest of waters from the stone chalice. "You've had quite a ride." One priest said with a smile. Quietly, Chuck smiled in the background and just waited there.

Sam was dusted off and was met by people who he hadn't seen in years. Carrying on small talk and truly thanking them, he also noticed something odd. In the corner of his eye, he, for the first time, he saw Heavenly souls who were largely invisible to him up to now.

"*Woah…*" He thought with widened eyes, "*Something has changed.*" They hovered above, smiled at him and he could hear them as clear as day. But no one else talking to Sam seemed to see them.

The Heavenly souls wished him the best of luck, told him of their pride in him and that they couldn't wait until he was with them. The absolute joy and love he felt was like that of constantly being held by an Angel.

But that feeling of absolute joy and love was still too overpowering to him. In all their splendor, he eventually had to shield his eyes from them. But he *was able* to see them directly for a while for the first time. Something he had never been able to do.

Sam knew it would still be a while before he was really ready to go up. Still, this achievement of self humility and forgiveness was a huge step. Sensing his backing off, the Heavenly souls evaporated in a shimmer.

He spotted Chuck after meeting with everyone and almost collapsed. "Please take me home." Sam said with an exhausted and weak smile. He crawled into the old car's back seat and was fast asleep before arriving home. Chuck got him home and left for the day.

Sam slept a sleep for the ages. His dreams were so vivid and beautiful that he was amazed at the intensity of them. However, one dream also showed Mike. And Mike needed his help.

Without waking, Sam found himself directly at Mike's side inside a cold, damp, dark bathroom. Mike was extremely drunk and had a razor pressed against his wrist. He was slowly opening the skin. Without even thinking, Sam knelt next to him and held his hand on the razor. Sam spoke softly and said the first thing that came to mind. A prayer that he knew well:

"I know I am not worthy to receive you, but only say the word….."

Mike also looked up with tears in his eyes. "God please help me."

Grabbing Mike's arm, Sam could now feel Mike's sorrow within himself. But he could also feel the sense of absolute joy and love that he had just acquired within himself. Without guidance or thought, Sam willed this feeling of peace into Mike.

Sam looked up. "Your will be done, but if I have gone through this for any reason, please let my peace go to him. I will do it all over again—for him."

For the very first time, love, peace and joy came directly outward from within himself. Without knowing how or why, he willed his own giving spirit into the young man. Mike fell over and sobbed. He slept for two full days. Sam did not leave his side.

When Mike woke up, he looked around entirely confused. The expected hangover was there, but not the usual feeling of soul wrenching emptiness. Some realization of what had happened hit him hard.

"Man, I almost screwed up real bad. I gotta get this under control- God. I will fix this." It was Mike's first real prayer. He first real sense of.... Peace.

Mike looked up and smiled. "Thank you."

"That's your second prayer Mikey, but who's counting." Sam said and smiled. Sam looked up and softly spoke. "Thank you."

Sam watched with a sense of immense pride in the new man. He knew that this truly was the young man's new beginning. A reborn soul came out of that house that day. Sam began to realize the similarities between them.

Only by Mike accepting that very same humility that Sam had just done and by trusting in something greater than himself, could he rise above it all.

Happily, Sam took one last look at Mike and thought of home.

"I think he's going to be alright for a while now." Sam arrived home to find the bell chiming in his mailbox." It was an invitation for a new arrival. It read that a new soul was on the way to Midtown straight away. It recommended that Sam see the priest at St. Michael's immediately for any questions.

Running franticly out of the main gate, he got there as fast as he could. The priest recognized Sam and the importance of the situation. He was unusually quick and to the point.

"She's in her log cabin now and resting comfortably. She will awake when you arrive. Do you want to be the one to guide her initially? We think you're ready."

"Me? Wait.... We?" He noticed that the same shimmering man with the sword was smiling slightly against the wall.

"We." The priest responded happily. "But you must hurry."

Sam smiled and nodded at the Angel. He started to walk, but it turned into a jog, then a dead run. As he ran down the street he heard the priest yelling. "And remember how to do the vision box! You're going to need it!"

Sam sprinted from Midtown and ran into the gate next store to his house. Through the portal, he saw a rustic log cabin located on a shimmering lakeside. He collected his thoughts as he stepped through.

"This is all happening so fast. Why me? Why now?"

Bracing himself with false bravado, he continued on slowly. He slowed down even more to walk up the front stairs. As he did so, he happened to glance into one of the rippled, hand blown glass windows and noticed his image. Not only did he now have a long blond beard, but that he was dressed in a flannel shirt, blue jeans and boots.

"Ok. This is freaking me out. Someone spent wayyy too much time in the woods.... Fine. I can do this." Sam whispered to no one.

He took a few steps forward and reached for the door handle.

"You know God. I have no idea what I'm doing. I can't do this." He whispered as he looked up.

He started to turn away and felt an immense feeling of joy shoot shivering down his spine. He could almost *feel* it emanating from his body. For the very first time, the joy didn't come from an Angel or from *her*. For the very first time the joy came from *within*.

"Gotcha. I can do this." He looked up, smirked and walked through the cabin's rough cut door cautiously. He stepped quietly inside the lantern lit room and closed the door behind him. A warm fire crackled in the fireplace on the far side. As he took it all in, he noticed a young woman stirring gently awake on a bed in the corner of the room.

"Where am I? What a dream I've had." she said and slowly looked around. "This place looks familiar, but who are you? Where am I?"

Sam smiled as he recognized her. Trying not act surprised, he gently sat down on a stool next to the bed and tried to pull himself together. He looked up and admired the young woman's perfect brown hair and chestnut eyes.

He was looking at a much younger version of his mother.

He glanced down next to the old wooden bed and saw a rolled up book laying on the night stand. Intrigued, he laid his hand on the weathered white book and recognized it as the same one that was hidden in his grandfather's back pocket when he first met him in the hospital room so long ago. The worn golden script read "The Midtown Express."

Through the open cabin window, a fresh breeze crept in. The familiar smell of fresh roses filled the room. Smirking with irony and feeling a renewed sense of purpose, Sam thought of what the old man had said to him. Clearing his throat, he leaned in.

"EXACTLY what do you remember? Tell me everything."

10% of the proceeds of this book will be given to charity.

(The Midtown Express)

ISBN: 978-0-615-55546-1

www.ingramcontent.com/pod-product-compliance
Lightning Source LLC
LaVergne TN
LVHW050935080826
845145LV00004B/1273

* 9 7 8 0 6 1 5 8 0 4 5 8 3 *